RISE OF THE SOVEREIGN GUARDIAN

JORDAN E KRISTOFER

Cover Composition by HSBookCovers

Cover Illustration by Nicholas Bueltel

1st edition 2025

For my family,
who always had faith in me,
even when I didn't.

CONTENTS

Simplified Qia Mora's Sword. The cross symbolizes the sword She used to fight the shiden, while the circle and dot symbolize the sun, which She is believed to inhabit.

1

LOST, THEN FOUND

T HERE WAS A TREMENDOUS storm making its way
through Geth Rell, causing shops in the city to
close. Rain echoed through the open cobblestone streets.
The street lamps were out, dowsed by the rain that seemed
to come from all directions.

This caused a particularly slow day at the Heid's Mirth
Tavern. The fire in the hearth kept a single man warm,
and round chandeliers hung low above patronless dining
tables. Indeed, the man was the only one left besides the
tavern-keeper and her daughter. According to local fore-
seers, the storm had stalled, resting angrily above the city.

The man was a priest, sipping tea contemplatively. He
was dressed in usual worship attire and wore a Mother's
Sword around his neck. His dark hair was of a good length,
tied into a small ponytail by a ribbon that saw great use.
The stubble on his hard jaw would have been shaved had
he held a congregation recently, and his dark eyes reflected

the dancing flames before him. The front door opened and closed unnoticed, but the thudding of dense leather heels periodically dropping a large suitcase broke his concentration. He looked up from the hearth's healthy blaze to search the source of the sound.

He found his eyes resting upon a figure cloaked in dark gray. A large hood sat at the top of the figure, and he could see the shape of a large crescent-shaped blade on its hip. The individual seemed to be having difficulty carrying the suitcase, being unable to keep it off the floor for much time. When it arrived at the front desk, he noticed its diminutive size, as if it were a mature girl. He watched as a gloved hand, dainty and slight, rang the bell on the counter several times, and then stood gravely still.

The priest realized he had slightly misjudged the figure's size when he saw the tavern-keeper walk up to it, standing over the figure's fragile frame, which seemed even shorter in comparison. The woman was relatively tall, just surpassing the priest's own height. Her chest was prominent in the bodice, made all the more conspicuous by a tight, lowborn corset. Her face showed a maturity gained in hardship, with her hair worn in likewise fashion.

"What can I do for you?" the tavern-keeper asked politely, giving a smile.

Though he had been there a while, the priest was consistently surprised by the tavern-keeper's manners; her politeness seemed to know no bounds.

"I would like a room," said a stern female voice that still had ample youth.

The tavern-keeper squinted in skepticism.

"Then, please, remove your hood," she said.

"No," replied the figure.

The tavern-keeper straightened in both posture and countenance.

"I'm sorry. But I don't deal in persons who keep their faces hidden."

The figure let out a quiet sigh neither the priest nor the tavern-keeper heard. It reached for the sides of its hood and pulled it back. A young feminine face was revealed. Her skin was a light blue, contrasting her long, bright yellow hair left loose, covering the sides of her face. Strikingly, she had large, dark horns that soared from the front of her temples up and back toward her neck, jutting out to the sides at their curving peaks. Green predator-like eyes gave her an odd, yet alluring, appearance.

The tavern-keeper received this revelation with surprise; she had not seen that kind in her tavern in some time. She stood closer to the counter, putting one hand on the counter and another on a concealed pistol under it.

"Do you have your free papers," she said, almost in a cautious manner.

The girl lifted her hair up from one side of her head to reveal her unblemished, round ear.

"Does *this* answer your question?" she asked with a straight face.

The tavern keep nodded.

"Yes."

She walked out from the counter and went behind a small wall. The girl put her hand on her crescent sword, but the tavern-keeper emerged armed only with a key attached to a wood tag.

"Room five is open."

"Thank you," the girl said, taking the key in her small hand.

She went to pull her hood up when the tavern-keeper stopped her.

"Excuse me," the woman said, "but no hoods allowed. As long as you're lodging."

The girl let her hood fall. The woman pointed at the suitcase.

"Do you need help with that?"

"No," said the girl. "I will be fine."

She walked up the stairs to the balcony overlooking the dining room, stepping the suitcase the whole way. The priest watched her movements as she walked out of sight toward her room. He looked back at the fire, this time in confusion.

A horned vedzryyf'len[1] ? Here? he thought. *Never thought I'd see one again.*

The tavern-keeper's feminine footfalls alerted the priest to her presence.

"May I join you, Father?" she asked.

"Be my guest," he replied, allowing the mature woman to sit in a chair next to him. "But I'm no longer a priest, ma'am."

"Oh? Why's that?"

"Eh, I'd rather not discuss it."

The woman nodded vigorously.

"Oh, I see. Holy matters for holy people."

The priest smirked and chuckled.

"Is that why you've been here for so long?"

"Well that...and the storm," the priest said.

"Oh, yes. The storm's been awful. It's been here quite a while."

"Indeed. Seems strange to me, though. Is this sort of storm normal?"

---

1. (vehj-REEF-lehn) Literally "moon people." They generally have characteristic blue skin, large horns, dark hair, and vertical slit pupils. Larger horns tend to indicate a more powerful vedzryyf'len. However, some have exceedingly small horns or none at all; these are common in Cormoria, but fully-horned vedzryyf'len are much more rare. All known vedzryyf'len are female; how their numbers continue to grow is a Mohnahti secret.

"The storm? Yes, it's normal. For this long? No. I can't recall this ever happening before."

"Strange."

"Yes, strange."

The two sat quietly for a moment, the priest sipping his tea and the tavern-keeper staring at the fire.

"*She's* a strange sight," spoke the tavern-keeper.

"That girl?"

"Mm-hm," nodded the woman.

"I thought the same. A horned vedzryyf'len in Geth Rell is a rare sight indeed."

"What's strange...she was never owned."

The priest looked at her.

"Never owned?" he said. "You mean she's *always* been free?"

"It seems that way."

"Now that *is* strange. *More* than strange."

"Spooky, some would say." The tavern-keeper paused. "Azurns[2] sure are wild."

The priest's brow furrowed briefly.

"Maybe she's here to recruit ones like her to fight out east."

"Perhaps," he paused. "Perhaps she's here on vacation."

"In *this* weather?"

---

2. A racial slur based on vedzryyf'len's ubiquitous blue skin. Translated loosely from the original to retain meaning.

"Visiting, maybe," he shrugged.

The sound of dense leather heels perked up the two interlocutors. They watched the girl as she walked down the stairs, her bare hand gliding down the railing. Her steps were strong such that if one were to just hear her footsteps, one would think she were a man.

She was dressed in a gray tunic with sleeves, a black leather belt cinched at the waist. Her gray pants were cut off by high black boots that showed barely any wear; she either kept them well or had just embarked on her journey. She walked over to the hearth, her eyes piercing through the two spectators.

"Could I please have something to eat?" she asked politely.

They looked at each other in amazement, then back at the girl.

"Yes. I can get you something," said the tavern-keeper.

She stood up and walked toward the kitchen. The girl and the priest looked at each other.

"May I?" she said, gesturing toward the chair.

"Go ahead," said the priest.

She walked around the chair and gently sat down. She had an unusually straight posture as she watched the frolicking flames.

"May I ask your name?" the priest said.

She was quiet for a moment.

"Dzokaya," the girl replied.

"My name's Pel," he said, smiling gently.

"Pleasure," she said, still looking at the fire.

Pel nodded.

"What is a young lady like you doing in Geth Rell? In a terrible storm, no less."

"You mean *someone* like me," she retorted.

"Well—"

Dzokaya abruptly turned toward him.

"I am *well* aware of the fate of my people here. But I am more than capable of fending for myself."

"I meant no offense, my child," he said in reflex.

"'My child.' I am *not* of your kin."

"I'm sorry...Dzokaya."

She gave a hearty nod.

"Indeed. Your Lady gives me *no* kindness."

"But She professes it."

"Yet She instructs your kind to treat mine with—"

"*She* does not. My fellow man does, and it's most unfortunate."

"To say the *least*," Dzokaya responded.

"Indeed." Pel paused. "It's why I left my order," he said, slumping into his chair in defeat.

"Unlikely," she scoffed.

"You know," Pel said, crossing his arms gently and speaking in a fatherly tone, "not all of us are as cruel as you may think. Some of us have a heart and would like nothing more than to see the liberation of your people."

"It remains to be seen."

"Perhaps where *you're* from, but not here. The slave trade's illegal here."

"And you expect me to take your word for it?" she asked.

There was a moment of silence.

"I suppose not," Pel said. "Perhaps in time."

"Perhaps," Dzokaya echoed.

More silence followed before the tavern-keeper came with the girl's food.

"Here you are," the woman said, holding it out to the girl, smiling.

"Thank you," the vedzryyf'len said, standing up to meet a bowl of stew.

She looked at the steaming brown contents with disappointment.

"Do you have anything more...desirable?" Dzokaya asked, looking up at the woman.

She raised an eyebrow.

"I'm sorry, but this is all there is," she said as if she were disappointed by her own explanation.

Dzokaya sighed.

"This will do," she said, taking the bowl in her delicate hands.

She was handed a spoon and a cloth napkin, and sat down in her chair. The tavern-keeper walked to the back.

With spoon in hand, Dzokaya dipped it into the bowl's dark depths and fished out a piece of meat and some vegetables. She sighed and pulled the spoon into her mouth. As she chewed, her eyebrows raised in surprised delight.

"Our commoner food isn't too bad, now is it?" asked Pel with a smug smirk.

She turned to him.

"What makes you say that?" she said.

"Your accent. You're a highborn."

"I suppose it is difficult to hide."

"Indeed, it is. Especially among us lowborn."

Pel leaned forward, placing his forearms on his knees.

"How'd a free horned vedzryyf'len become a highborn, I wonder," he said.

"I am not one to divulge personal history to a *strange* priest I met in some *old* tavern," Dzokaya replied.

"Of course," Pel said, leaning back into his chair. "But it *is* a question many will ask as you stay here."

"What 'many'? There is nary a person here."

"You won't be staying here the *whole* time, I presume. You're bound to meet other people who'll wonder the same question. Perhaps even ask it outright. Either way, you're an offense to their lifestyle."

"An offense?" she said in insulted protest.

"'Offense' might be too strong, but Geth Rell is not known to house many horned ones, much less have them highborn. People are bound to stare."

"What do you propose?" Dzokaya asked, eating another spoonful.

Pel smirked.

"A priest whom they trust would surely ease tensions," he said.

"Oh, no. You are *not* following me around like some... *child*."

"Are you not one?"

"I will have you know I have seen twenty summers."

"Twenty? How 'bout that?" Pel laughed. "I'd've taken you for *less*."

"What? Do I not look my age?"

He chuckled.

"Not at all. When you pulled your hood off, I thought you skipped school."

Dzokaya huffed and scowled at the comment.

"But you have a sword," Pel said, "and that counts for something, I guess."

"It certainly does," she said before eating another spoonful.

"I assume you know how to use it, then."

The girl nodded heartily.

"I do," she said between chews.

"Well, that's better than most people."

She swallowed.

"Do *you* have skill with a sword?"

"Used to," Pel replied. "I've not held a sword in some time. Ever since I became a priest."

He put a hand to his chin in thought.

"I guess it wouldn't be *too* hard picking it back up," he said to himself.

Thunder rolled outside, and the rain came down hard. Pel looked up at the ceiling when the rain briefly intensified, and then looked at the window. He stood up, the chair creaking slightly, and put his tea on a nearby table. He walked to the window.

Deep puddles had formed among the cobblestones, and the scant trees had lost many of their leaves despite being well into spring. The dark clouds above caused the area below to be nearly pitch black. The only indications of a city outside the tavern were highlights of the buildings from intermittent lightning flashes.

Pel sighed and walked back to his chair. He picked up his tea and took a sip. Then, he looked up at the clock near the hearth.

"It's getting late," he said to himself.

"Is it?" said Dzokaya.

"Almost eleven." He looked back at her. "It must be passed your bedtime."

Dzokaya swallowed another spoonful.

"I am an adult. I have no bedtime," she shot back.

Pel smiled and chuckled again.

"You're a highborn, alright. Don't know when to take a joke."

She huffed and sat back forcefully into her chair. The priest began to walk away.

"Goodnight, Dzokaya. May She grant you pleasant dreams," he said as he walked out of sight to his room.

Dzokaya was not sure whether Pel referred to his Mother or hers, but she accepted the blessing all the same.

As she sat in her chair, she looked into her stew as if she expected to find the answer to end her journey. Her meditations had guided her to Geth Rell in pursuit of her parents' killer. The storm beckoned her, but now it clouded her perception; it seemed the whole city was blanketed in the evil energy she was following. It was neither of her Lady nor Pel's, but something wholly different. *Is this the power from ancient times?* she thought. Her mother told her stories about then, but a time before Them seemed far fetched to say the least.

"Ar'ka Mohn[3], guide me," Dzokaya said to herself.

Her horns buzzed as if to signify She had heard her plea. Dzokaya touched one of her horns in response, then dragged her hand along its length in contemplation.

Fully-horned vedzryyf'len were exceedingly rare in Corlia[4], and Dzokaya knew this.

---

3. (AHR-kah MOHN) Known to humans as the Shadow Mistress, Creator of the vedzryyf'len and the nation of Mohnaht. She is believed to inhabit the moon.

4. A nation in southeast Cormoria, where the vedzryyf'len slave trade is alive and well.

Her physical features were a focus during day-to-day interactions. Most Corlians had seen enslaved, nearly-hornless vedzryyf'len, but ones who had fully-grown, long horns were more rare than Gek'reken feathers[5].

Dzokaya was intent on keeping a low profile while she was in Geth Rell proper, but it would be difficult since she knew she was bound to interact with people in her search.

Who could have the strength to kill father and mother?

It must have been a very powerful magister[6], but the presence she followed was nothing like one; it was more like an amorphous, malevolent entity that chilled her to her bones. It gnawed at her soul, attempting to consume it. It was angry, but it cackled in vicious glee. It was a feeling she had never felt before, and her mother never told her of such a thing.

Perhaps mother did not know such a thing existed.

The girl managed to maintain her guard against this presence. If she felt it, she reasoned, then Pel most certainly would as well; he was a priest, after all.

---

5. A saying roughly equivalent to "rare as hen's teeth." Although hen's teeth don't exist, Gek'reken (GEHK-rehk-ehn) will sprout feathers at an advanced age. While their ages can extend into the thousands-of-years, those with feathers are known to be the oldest (and rarest) of their people, believed to be older than the events in the Uch Rynahl.

6. Someone who is enlisted in a nation's meigys-using army. Those who are considered meigys-using mercenaries (or those generally not bound to an official force) are called "mages."

Dzokaya stood and turned with her stew, then headed for the staircase.

When she got to the top, she slowly walked down the hall and looked at the bottom of each door, searching for light.

She saw light coming through the top and bottom of a door toward the end of the hall and walked toward it. When she reached the door, she stopped and thought for a moment.

Perhaps he is getting ready for bed. Maybe I should not bother him.

She turned, and as she started to walk away, the door opened.

"Oh," Pel said. "Can I help you?"

The two looked at each other.

"May I come in?" Dzokaya asked with concern in her voice.

"Yes. Yes, of course," said Pel as he opened the door further and stepped aside to let her in.

She still held the bowl of stew in her hands; it was keeping them warm.

The room was about the size of hers. It housed a full bed and a small table with two chairs. An oil lamp rested on the table. Dzokaya pulled out the chair closest to the door and sat down, placing the bowl on the table. Pel closed the door and sat down in the opposite chair.

"What can I do for you...Dzokaya?"

She remained silent, as if stewing over a grudge, and then spoke.

"Have you felt...a presence?" she asked.

"A presence?"

She stood up abruptly.

"Never mind. It is just my imagination."

"No, it isn't. Sit down, please."

She looked at him with his concerned face and sat back down.

"I have felt...*something*. A presence, I'm not sure. It feels more like a...a," he said, looking for the word. "A dark sludge."

The girl squinted, trying to understand what he meant.

"It's like everything here is slowed down, like in a mire. Dark, depressing, *sadness*. I've not felt much like it before."

"'*Much* like it'? You have felt it before?"

"Something similar. Yes."

"Do you know what it is?"

"I wish I could tell you. But no, I don't. As I said, I've felt something *like* it before during my soldiering days."

"What was it?"

"We never found out. Or rather, *I* never found out."

"You were alone?"

"Sort of. I was the only one who felt it." Pel paused. "I'm not sure why *I* was alone in it, but I know what I experienced."

"Did you search for it?"

Pel scoffed.

"No. I was a soldier on duty, not a gallivanting paladin. I couldn't do things I wasn't ordered to do, much less follow a foggy feeling of unease and darkness. But I've felt it a few more times since then."

"Under what circumstances?"

"Ah, I don't know. *Random* ones, if I'm to be honest. Once out in a field, another in several of my parishioners' homes. *Another* in a church. And now here."

Pel sat back in his chair, hands clasped together on the table in front of him. There was silence.

"I have been tracking this...feeling, as you say, for a while," Dzokaya said. "It was in Kir Mysch[7] —"

"You came from Kir Mysch?"

"Yes. That is where I live."

"Well, you're far from home."

"It is also where my parents were murdered."

"Murdered?"

She nodded. Pel rubbed his stubble.

"And you think this feeling — this presence — is responsible?" he asked.

"I do."

Pel leaned forward onto the table.

---

7. A popular port on the southwestern shores of Corlia. It is a main port for the vedzryyf'len slave trade.

"Be straight with me, child," he said. "Where under Heaven do you hail from?"

"I told you. Kir Mysch."

"No. Who are your *parents*?"

Dzokaya went quiet.

"You're a horned *free* vedzryyf'len who's *also* a highborn. These things are not common. Nor do they make sense."

Dzokaya looked intently at her cooling bowl of stew. The vegetables and meat had sunk to the bottom, and the fat floating on top of the broth began to congeal. She took it as a sign.

"My...father," she started, "was highborn. My mother...was the chieftess of a tribe in Mohnaht[8]. She was taken as a slave, and my father found her when she came into port. He bought her freedom, and she felt indebted to him." Dzokaya paused. "They fell in love," she said, shrugging. "And they had me."

Pel sat leaning back in his chair, arms folded.

"You said they were murdered," he said.

Dzokaya nodded.

"Yes. By something evil."

"The same presence you feel here?"

---

8. (Mohn-AHT) A nation to the south of Cormoria that is the home of all vedzryyf'len. It was formed when Ar'ka Mohn planted the Ar'ka Tree on an isolated island, which grew to form the nation as it is today.

"Yes."

Pel sighed.

"Do you have a bearing on it?" he asked.

"No. I feel it all around me. As if the storm itself were the presence."

"Hmph. Then we're of a like mind." He paused. "Any idea where to start looking?"

Dzokaya slumped back into her chair, as if she were disappointed in herself.

"No. I came here to collect my thoughts. A change of scenery, as they say."

There was silence between the two.

Dzokaya suddenly felt very vulnerable. She had not told anyone her lineage, but there was something about Pel that made her tell him the truth.

She had lied to others before, including those within her parents' circles. She was a child Kir Mysch — and Corlia as a whole — would not accept. She was worse off than the child of a slave: the sight of her prominent horns rose fear in those who had even the slightest idea of true vedzryyf'len power. Indeed, the stories of legions of shiden[9] losing to handfuls of vedzryyf'len shamans gave people a reason to fear them. Whether they were true or not did not matter.

---

9. (shee-DEHN, singular SHEED) Demon-like entities created by the corrupting power of Yych Rehe.

But perhaps it was Pel's being a priest that made her feel comfortable with him.

Pel looked at the clock next to his bed. It was almost midnight. He pinched the bridge of his nose and rubbed his eyes.

"It's late," he said, rising out of his chair. "We should discuss this in the morning. Sleep on it, you know?"

Dzokaya nodded.

"Of course. Rest will do us good," she said, standing up and grabbing her stew.

"Indeed. Might also want to eat up," Pel paused. He walked over to the girl and put his hand on her head. "Nutrition will help you grow."

Dzokaya turned in anger and stormed out of the room; all the while, Pel had a smirk on his face.

2

OLD FRIENDS, NEW ALLIES

LIGHTNING FLASHES LIT DZOKAYA'S room as she slept. Her horns propped her head up slightly off her pillow. As she lay in bed, a knocking came from her door. She pulled the blanket up over her head in a failed attempt to block out the noise.

When the knocking continued, she threw the blanket off her face and sighed. She then sat up and moved the blankets down off her legs.

The girl stood up in her nightgown and went over to the door. She opened it, and Pel's grim face greeted her.

"Morning," he said in a sullen tone.

"Good morning," Dzokaya groggily replied. "What time is it?"

"Almost eight."

She sighed.

"Could you not let me sleep?"

"I could, but we've got more important matters."

"Hm?"

"There's been a strange death nearby."

The half-breed perked up.

"I was going to investigate myself, but you know more about this presence than I do." He paused. "Shall we?"

"Yes. Let me get dressed," Dzokaya replied.

"Right."

She closed the door, and Pel turned slightly in thought.

"Twenty summers?" He scoffed. "I doubt it."

He walked away down the hall.

A dressed Dzokaya met him in the main room of the tavern.

"How did you come about this knowledge?" she asked Pel.

"An officer stopped by for a meal. We got to talking, and he told me."

Afterward, they walked in relative silence in the rain on the way to the body.

When they arrived, the body of a man lay slumped in a corner between two buildings. It was oddly out in the open on a frequented street. The body was in a strange shape; it appeared as though it was dehydrated, eyes shriveled inside deep sockets and skin clinging heartily to muscleless bone. Its skin was pale and dry-looking despite the torrential rain.

Two constables stood guard to keep an invisible crowd at bay, and a third was examining the body.

Pel stepped forward in his priestly attire.

"Gentlemen," said Pel, nodding at the two lightly-armored men.

One of them put his hand up.

"I'm sorry, Father. No one is allowed near it," the constable sternly said.

"I was sent here to offer last rites to the deceased, Officer."

"We weren't aware the Order knew."

"They do. We just didn't have enough time to send a missive."

Pel's face was straight, projecting a certain earnestness. After a moment, the two officers stepped aside.

As Pel walked past them, Dzokaya began to follow, but the constables stopped her.

"Officers! She's my aide," Pel said. "She helps me with the rites."

The two eased and let Dzokaya pass, the darkness hiding her vedzryyf'len features.

Pel knelt down beside the constable examining the body.

"Officer," said Pel as a greeting.

"Father," replied the other.

"What do we have here?"

"A prune of a corpse, I'm afraid. Man looks like he spent too much time in the desert. Doesn't make sense. The rain and all."

"If I may, sir. I'd like to administer last rites."

"Of course, Father. I'll let you be."

The constable stood up and walked past Dzokaya. He glanced at her in her large hood, but he failed to recognize her heritage.

She knelt down next to Pel as he held the Mother's Sword around his neck, made the Sign of the Mother, and began to pray.

"Strange," Dzokaya said.

Pel nodded as he prayed.

Dzokaya touched the body with her gloved hand. Pel made the Sign of the Mother again and released his Sword.

"The work of your quarry?" he asked.

Dzokaya lifted the man's head and observed what used to be his eyes.

"It looks like it. It is eerily similar to how I found my parents, except they were not alone."

"Hm?"

"They were together...holding hands."

"I'm not sure if that's romantic or sad."

"Perhaps both."

Dzokaya took off one of her gloves and touched the man's cheek with her bare hand. Her brow furrowed.

"What is it?" Pel asked.

"His meigys[1] ."

---

1. (MAY-gihs) An energy that exists within all things and allows those who can control it to use powerful abilities and perform superhuman acts.

"What about it?"

"It is all there. I thought my eyes were deceiving me, but I was wrong."

"I don't understand."

"Are you not a meigys user?"

"No."

Dzokaya retracted her hand and put her glove back on.

"Meigys is in everything," Dzokaya said. "It keeps us alive. When we die, we lose all of it to the environment, replenishing the natural source."

"But his is still in his body?"

"Correct. He should still be alive."

"But he's clearly dead."

"Yes," Dzokaya said, nodding. She put a hand to her forehead in thought. "I must be missing something."

"Maybe he died another way. Like, uh, blood loss or something."

Dzokaya unsheathed her large crescent sword and dragged the edge along the crease of the corpse's elbow. Blood slowly oozed out from the shriveled flesh.

"So much for that idea," Pel said to himself.

Dzokaya looked up at him as if she had just had an idea.

"Where is the library?" she asked wide-eyed.

"Why?" Pel said, his brow lowered in confusion.

"I think it might have the answer I seek."

"Fair enough. I'll take you there."

Dzokaya sheathed her sword and stood up.

"We had better hurry," she said. "The rain is soaking through my clothes."

The pair looked diligently for a coach to ride to the library, but the constant downpour kept potential riders inside their homes for fear of getting drenched, which in turn caused the cabbies to not have much of a reason to do their jobs. Thus, Pel and Dzokaya walked quickly in the dark rain to Geth Rell's library.

Before long, the rain was too much for them to bare; their clothes quickly became waterlogged, and the lack of warm sun rays made sure the cold deluge stayed on them. Dzokaya shivered on the way, wrapping her arms around herself in a vain attempt to keep warm. From his days in the military, Pel was used to uncomfortable weather, but the sight of Dzokaya behind him struggling to keep warm tugged at his heart.

He stopped walking to allow Dzokaya to catch up, and he turned to her.

"We should go back," he said.

"No," Dzokaya said, still holding herself. "We *have* to get there."

"It's still some ways off."

"How much further?" she said, looking up at him.

Pel took out a pocket watch from his robes and opened it.

"At this rate, it'll be a while," he said, his face showing clear concern for Dzokaya's well-being.

The girl sighed.

"Is there somewhere we could go to warm up?" she asked as she looked about herself.

Pel looked up at a street sign and smiled.

"Yes. I know someone around here. With me!" Pel said, waving Dzokaya along.

A white owl followed them unseen.

Fortunately, the place Pel had in mind was not far. Within moments, they arrived.

The house was one of many in this particular residential district. It had stone walls that were reinforced with a stonetimber[2] cross. The second floor hung over the first, partially overhanging the street.

Pel used the knocker on the heavy wooden door. He made sure to use enough strength for the knock to be heard through the rain. The window next to the door was covered by twill curtains, and the small window in the door was meigysally blurred on the outside.

He saw the light in the window of the door dim slightly. Then it opened.

Before the two wet rags was a tall, lean man. He wore a simple shirt that was slightly opened to allow his skin to breathe, and his pants were rough. The man had a bony face, whose angles were further exaggerated by a large tri-

---

2. An extremely strong wood that is often used in the construction of buildings.

angular nose that ended in a sharp point. His brow was raised in surprise.

"Pel?" said the man. "What insanity is this?"

"We'd like to dry off, if you don't mind," said Pel, gesturing to the freezing Dzokaya.

The man looked at her with wide eyes for a moment before he nodded.

"Right. Right. Come in," he said, stepping aside to let them in. "Toya! Put up the bath! We've got guests!"

"Guests?" said a distant woman's voice. "In *this* weather?"

"It's Pel!" the man said as he closed the door.

"Oh, Father, forgive me!" said the woman over the sound of rushed footsteps. "I'll have it hot in a shot."

The man turned to the others.

"Sadly, I've no clothes for her," he said.

"What about your daughter's," suggested Pel.

There was a short silence.

"Perhaps," said the man. He looked at the girl. "I'm Kyf."

"If you don't mind," said Pel, "I'd like her to warm up first."

"Aye." Kyf turned to her. "You must be chilled to the bone. Follow me."

As Kyf led Dzokaya to the staircase, he stopped and turned to Pel.

"Make yourself at home, my friend."

The two men smiled at each other before Kyf escorted Dzokaya up to the bath, and Pel began to undress by the hearth. As he stripped, he noticed the Mother's Sword he had given them above the door.

Kyf and Dzokaya were silent on the way up. When they reached the doorway, he turned around to her, who craned her neck to look up at the comparatively halberd-like man.

"Stay here a minute," Kyf said before he opened the bathroom door and closed it.

The half-breed stood outside hearing murmuring behind the door. Suddenly, the door opened, and Kyf walked up to her.

"My wife, Toya, will help you," he said.

Dzokaya stepped into the bathroom, and Kyf closed the door behind her.

She was met by a woman in traditional attire, her sleeves rolled up. Her hands were clasped together at her waist, whose politeness was matched by a small, welcoming smile. Her hazel eyes were equally kind and inviting — as was a requirement for a proper housewife. Her light brown hair was tied into a tight bun.

"Oh my," she said, "*yer* different from what I was expectin'."

"Which was?" replied Dzokaya.

"Not one with such *big* horns. Nor one so pretty."

Dzokaya blushed a faint lavender and smiled.

"Thank you," she said.

"Course. Come, come, come," Toya said, waving the girl closer. "We've gotta get those wet clothes off ya before ye catch cold."

Meanwhile, as Kyf descended the stairs, Pel was undressing. His underwear was also sopping wet, and as he removed it, Kyf walked to the back room. He emerged shortly after with a simple shirt and pants.

"Here," Kyf said. "These should fit you. They're my brother's."

Pel smiled.

"Thanks," he said. "I appreciate you taking us in without notice. The Mother[3] would be proud."

Kyf walked around to a cushioned chair and sat down.

"Don't worry about it. You've done us so much good before, I couldn't turn you away." Kyf placed his ankle on his opposite knee and leaned back. "But I've gotta ask... what're you doing with *her?*" Kyf said, pointing up at the ceiling.

"We have a common goal," Pel said as he stood closer to the fire to dry off.

"And that would be?"

"We're trying to find the source of this storm."

Kyf raised an eyebrow in confusion.

---

3. Qia Mora (kee-uh MOR-uh). Worshipped as the Mother of Mankind and creator of the paladins. She is believed to rule the solar Heaven, where all humans go when they die.

"It's just a storm, Pel. It'll pass over soon enough."

"How long's it been here? Three — four days?"

"At least. Why?"

"Don't you think that awfully strange?"

"Eh," Kyf shrugged. "I'm not one to question Her ways. But I understand if *you* do." He chuckled. "That's practically your job."

Pel nodded and stepped away from the fire to put on the shirt and pants Kyf had brought him.

"But if it's as suspicious as you say, why have the vedzryyf'len girl join you?" Kyf asked. "It wouldn't be of *her* Lady's design. Would it?"

"We suspect it's of neither's."

"Neither?"

Pel nodded.

"Neither ours nor her Lady would set a storm overhead with such—" He stood holding the shirt in thought. "Such melancholy," Pel finally explained.

"Melancholy?"

"Yes."

"That doesn't sound like Her in the slightest."

"Neither is it Ar'ka Mohn. Both are not known to be negative entities." Pel put on the shirt. "Come to think of it, I recently read of a new conjecture that states they were lovers."

"Lovers?"

"Yes. I'd like to read it, if I could get my hands on it."

"D'you know who came up with it?"

"The head of theology up there at the university," said Pel, pointing behind himself with his thumb.

"Professor Hordynfyrt?!"

Pel shrugged.

"If that's his name, I'd like to speak with him," he said. "Although, he's probably a busy man."

"You're a priest, Pel. Must I remind you of that?"

"Ah, not anymore, I'm afraid."

Kyf took his ankle off his knee and sat up straight, grasping the arms of his chair firmly in surprise.

"What? Why?"

"While I was having a conversation with one of my brothers, he made a statement that...turned out to be true."

"Which was?"

Pel stood quietly.

"My order has been...*dabbling* in the vedzryyf'len slave trade," Pel managed to say.

"Dabbling?" Kyf echoed.

"Yes. Dabbling," Pel said, nodding quickly.

"So...what? They sell *one* slave instead of *five?*"

"I don't know," the former priest said, raising his hands in disgust and plopping down on an opposite chair. "The whole thing seemed strange."

"I'd say. Though I'm sure the highborn are fine with it."

"As far as I know," Pel replied before giving a hefty sigh. "Worship's gotten so complicated these days. My parents would never stand for it if they knew what *I* do."

"Something tells me it's always been complicated," Kyf replied. "I just think you can see it now."

"Perhaps." Pel leaned back in thought. "Had I known what I know now, I'd've left Geth Rell altogether," he said. "Go preaching to whoever would listen."

"Will preach for remda[4]," Kyf mocked.

Pel chuckled.

The two men were quiet for a moment.

"So, what's her name?" asked Kyf.

"Hm? Who?"

"The vedzryyf'len girl."

"Oh. Dzokaya."

Kyf gave a long nod.

"Traditional vedzryyf'len name," he remarked.[5]

"I suppose. Haven't met many of them to know."

"I've known a few. All free, now, thank the Mother."

"Strangely, though, she's a highborn...from Corlia."

"A *Corlian highborn?* How's *that* happen?"

"Her mother married into it."

---

4. (REHM-dah) The international currency of Cormoria.

5. Kyf is remarking on the fact that the "dz" sound (a "j" sound) is typical of (and almost exclusive to) vedzryyf'len names.

"Fascinating!"

Pel looked at the floor in thought.

"I'd sure like to see that conjecture," he said to himself.

"Later, my friend."

Pel looked up at Kyf as he got to his feet.

"Your clothes aren't the *slightest* bit dry, yet."

Kyf walked away and went to a nearby bookcase. He pulled a metal rod with hooks and a short rod on either end. As he walked over to the hearth, Pel grabbed his clothes off the floor. Kyf then secured the two hooks into holes in the mantle above the fireplace, and Pel quickly moved to put his drenched clothes on the rod.

"I can't thank you enough," Pel said as he straightened his clothes.

"Don't mention it," Kyf replied. "We've always been there for each other. This time's no different."

The priest smiled.

"Remember in the summer, years ago, when we were all so hot, we just jumped into the lake with our armor on?" he asked.

Kyf chuckled.

"Commander Medlo was *furious*," he said. "He thought our armor would rust."

"It did, though. Didn't it?"

The two men's chuckling turned into laughter.

"Aye."

Dzokaya sat in the warm bath with a washcloth. Toya had been trying to make idle chit-chat with her.

"What is that laughter about?" the girl said, turning her head toward the door.

"Oh, don't mind them," Toya replied. " They're probably reminiscin' 'bout the army,"

Dzokaya turned to look at the woman.

"They fought together?" she asked.

"Fought?" Toya laughed. "Those two were mostly supply movers." She put a finger to her chin. "But I do remember Pel bein' good with a sword. Course, that was *years* ago."

Dzokaya gave a long nod, her horns nearly touching the bath as she did so. She then breathed deep and dunked her head under the water. The bath made a dull clang sound. She stayed submerged for a moment, then came up for air.

"I hate when that happens," she said.

"Sounded like it hurt," said Toya.

"Not quite. It is just a pulling feeling."

"Oh."

"It is just embarrassing."

"Especially in front 'a people ye just met, I'm sure."

The girl nodded.

"Oh, don't be embarrassed, sweety," Toya said, chuckling while taking a washcloth and dunking it into the bath water. "We've all done thin's we wish we hadn't in front 'a people."

Toya put her hand on Dzokaya's shoulder to have her lean forward so she could wash the girl's back.

"Why, I remember when I met Kyffi," said Toya, smiling. "I was kicked by a cow in ta the mud in front 'a him while he was patrollin' ma town. He helped me up, but I was so covered in mud, when he saw me clean, he didn't recognize me." Toya laughed.

Dzokaya smiled and started washing her legs.

"How old are ya, sweety?"

Dzokaya's smiled straightened.

"Old enough," she replied.

"For what?"

"To be on my own. Pel already commented on how young I look."

"Oh, don't mind him. I'm sure he was just jokin'."

"He *did* say I did not know how to take a joke."

"Well, all you highborns're so serious all the time, it's hard to believe any 'a ya have fun, let alone joke around."

"Is my accent *that* noticeable?"

"Course. Quite hard to hide it, I'm sure." Toya paused. "Now, do ya need help with ye horns, or do ya got 'em on yer own?"

"I can do them. Thank you."

Dzokaya wrapped the washcloth around one of her horns and slid the cloth along its length; she had to bend her neck and arm a certain way in order for her to reach their tips.

Toya watched in piqued interest. The presence of the half-breed allowed her to learn much about vedzryyf'len.

After she cleaned both her horns, she continued with the rest of herself.

"Do ya ever wish ya didn't have 'em?" Toya asked.

Dzokaya looked into Toya's eyes and smiled slightly, their kindness sinking in.

"Sometimes," she said. "I often wonder whether they are a blessing or a curse. Every time I think they are one, they become the other."

"I think they're lovely."

Dzokaya's meek smile widened.

"Thank you," she said before returning to washing.

"Ye mighty welcome. From what *I've* heard, they ought ta always be a blessin'. Havin' power like that?" Toya said, shaking her head slightly. "I can only imagine. But we humans can only *dream* of meigys like that."

"Indeed. Vedzryyf'len meigys is very potent. But your best paladins[6] can match it, I have heard."

"Really?" said Toya. "Maybe. I'd have ta ask the boys."

"They're paladins?"

"Oh, Heavens, no," Toya said, chuckling. "But they *have* watched 'em."

---

6. A powerful warrior blessed by Qia Mora and imbued with Her power.

"I see," Dzokaya said, giving a long nod. "I would like to be present during that conversation."

"I'll make sure ye are."

Suddenly, there was a knock on the door.

"Who is it?" Toya responded.

"It's Pel!"

"Do not come in!" said Dzokaya.

"I just wanted to make sure you were alright."

"Oh, we're fine, Pel!" Toya said, sitting up straight on the stool. "She'll be out soon, you silly priest!"

"Alright! Alright!" Pel said through the door. "Kyf and I'll be waiting in the den for breakfast, then."

The sound of fading footsteps allowed Dzokaya to lean back in the bath.

"If he saw me...*naked*, I would never hear the end of it," she said.

"Wha'da ya mean?" Toya asked with a furrowed brow.

"He thinks I am a child enough as it is."

"Are ye not?"

Dzokaya's eyes widened in embarrassed surprise.

"I am twenty, ma'am," she said in a stern tone.

Toya put her hands up in submission.

"Pardon *me*, then, young'n. I didn't mean te offend."

Dzokaya sighed.

"Is *that* what's got ya?" asked Toya. "Ya want ta show him ye not a child?"

"He must not think that way of me," the girl responded, fists slowly clenching under the bath water.

"Well, ta be honest, ya *do* look very young, dear. Maybe if ya...developed more, he might not think yer a child."

Dzokaya sighed again, releasing her fists. A sudden sadness washed over her, and Toya knew to change the subject.

"Let's finish gettin' ya washed. Then I'll get ya some nice, warm clothes. I should have some from ma daughter's wardrobe."

As Pel descended the stairs, Kyf looked up to see him shaking his head.

"What's wrong?" Kyf asked.

"I think I embarrassed her," Pel said.

"Toya?"

"Dzokaya."

"Oh, pfft. Don't worry about the girl," Kyf said, leaning back in his chair. "She needs to lighten up."

"Right, but—"

"She's a highborn, Pel. They get embarrassed if their house azurn misplaced the table settings."

"Point taken," Pel said, sitting down in the chair opposite Kyf.

The two veterans sat mute for a while, both staring at the fire drying Pel's clothes. As the fire began to die, Kyf stood up and dropped another log onto the remains, sending embers up into the flue. Pel looked up at a portrait of a young girl on the mantle.

His brow furrowed.

"How long's it been?" Pel asked, pointing up casually at the photograph.

"It'll be two years next month," Kyf said.

Pel let out a sad sigh.

"How's Toya holding up?"

"She has her moments." Kyf paused. "That vedzryyf'len girl you brought here is sure to stir up something of Liora," he said, pointing behind himself with his thumb.

"You sure?"

"Aye. The girl's practically the same size *she* was."

"True."

The feminine sound of heeled boots followed by a young man's footsteps echoed from the second floor. Before long, Toya and Dzokaya were walking down the stairs.

"Well?" Toya asked, stepping aside for the men to get a view of the girl. "Wha'da ye think?"

Dzokaya stood with her hands folded below her waist, dressed in a light blue button-down dress with a white lace collar. The frills of the skirt went down just below her knees, exposing molasses-colored tights and dark leather boots. She reminded Pel of a girl he had courted in his youth before he enlisted in the Geth Rell army, though Dzokaya appeared to have more innocence than the girl he had known.

Pel smiled.

"Pretty," he said.

Dzokaya looked down at the floor trying to ignore a lavender blush across her cheeks.

"Thank you," she said.

"Reminds me of—" Kyf said before he cut himself off; he could see the tears welling up in his wife's eyes. "Reminds me of breakfast," he said, rising to his feet. "Darling, you should prepare breakfast."

Toya sniffled slightly and nodded.

"Aye," she said. "O' course."

The couple walked out of the den to the kitchen. Pel put his hand out.

"Come," he said, waving her closer. "Take a seat by the fire."

Dzokaya walked slowly to the chair Kyf was sitting in and lowered herself gently into it. As she looked into the fire, Pel saw a different side of her. The orange light of the fire mixed with her colored features, creating a deeply-olive southerner. In this guise, he thought she made a pretty human.

The vedzryyf'len girl sat politely — as her governess had taught her — and looked up from the fire when she heard the sound of plates clattering in the kitchen. She looked back at the doorway and turned to Pel.

"Do they own this house?" she asked innocently.

Pel's brow furrowed.

"Of course," he replied. "Why?"

"But they are cooking breakfast themselves?"

"Right."

"Do they not have staff to do it for them?"

Pel gave a big smile.

"The lowborn do things themselves, mostly," he said, holding back a laugh. "Most don't have the wealth to...*buy* people to do things for them."

She looked down at the area rug between them.

"It is a strange way to live," she said.

"As is yours to us," Pel replied, leaning back and folding his arms.

Her gaze was drawn back to him.

"I suppose it's a good thing I brought us here."

"Why is that?"

"You get to see the other side."

Dzokaya suddenly felt very embarrassed, and the lavender that had appeared before came back stronger.

3

— • —

THEORY CRAFTING

A s Dzokaya and Pel walked through the pocket
door into the kitchen, they were struck by the smell
of breakfast breads and meats. Toya was pulling scrambled
eggs from a skillet into a bowl, while Kyf sat at the head
of a table. It was set with four place settings, and plates of
pancakes, bacon, and breakfast sausages were in the middle
with a large bottle of milk near Kyf.

As the pair crossed the threshold, Kyf looked up from
his newspaper.

"Just in time, you two," he said.

"Must've been the smell," said Toya, bringing the bowl
of eggs to the table. "Come an' eat. Ye must be starvin'."

"I *am* hungry," Dzokaya said to herself as Pel pulled out
a seat for her by the near wall.

She sat down as he pushed it in under her. Pel sat at the
foot of the table as Toya sat closest to the stove.

Dzokaya pulled the napkin from under the silverware and placed it in her lap. She then held up her plate to be served. Toya and Kyf looked at her confusedly.

"We should give thanks first," said Kyf, looking at Pel.

The priest smirked at him, and the girl laid her plate back on the table.

They took their hands into each others, and they bowed their heads, eyes closed.

Pel took a breath.

"Thank you, Great Mother, for the bounty before us. May You forever provide for us, Your children. En teth[1]."

There was a moment of silence before Pel opened his eyes and smiled at Dzokaya.

"*Now*, we can eat," he said.

The group released their grips and started to serve each other in relative peace. Once they all filled their plates, Toya spoke up.

"So, where do ya hail from, Dzokaya?" she asked as she cut into a flapjack.

The girl swallowed a piece of sausage.

"Kir Mysch."

"Oh my."

---

1. (EHN tehth) Literally "in truth." Equivalent to saying "amen" after a prayer.

"What brings you halfway across Cormoria[2], child?" asked Kyf.

Dzokaya explained her situation, and a solemn silence rose in the room. Only Pel continued to eat.

"That brings us to the storm," said the priest, still looking down as he cut his food.

"The storm?" said Toya.

"Yes," Dzokaya nodded. "The storm is *filled* with the same presence I felt when my parents died."

"You feel it, too, then, Pel?" Kyf asked.

He nodded.

"Living up to your namesake, I see."[3] Kyf turned to the half-breed. "I have a question, though. Did you follow the presence, or did you follow the storm?"

"What do you mean?"

"If the storm's filled with this presence, then it might be that the storm's created *by* it. Was there a storm over Kir Mysch when your parents died?"

"A small one," Dzokaya said. "But not nearly as thick with sadness and anger."

---

2. The continent on which the majority of human nations exist, in which Geth Rell is a major port city. Translated as "Land of the Mother's Children."

3. Kyf is referencing the fact that "pel" is actually his nickname, which is an ancient Pyrmian word for "seer."

"Perhaps it's based off population," said the former priest. "Kir Mysch isn't as large a city as Geth Rell."

"What's the census say of the two?" asked Kyf.

"The Geth Rell Gazette said something like a million," said Pel. "A bit over, if I recall correctly."

"Kir Mysch is what? Half that?"

"Thereabout."

"But it's *huge*," said Toya.

"True," Kyf said. "Kir Mysch is more spread out."

"It is less dense than here."

"She has a point," Pel said. "Kir Mysch may cover more land, but it doesn't have *nearly* as many streets as here, nor are they as narrow."

"But to my point," Kyf said. "The storm might draw off people's negative emotions. The more people, the stronger the storm. Kir Mysch has fewer people, hence a smaller, weaker storm."

"Sound theory," agreed Pel.

"Indeed," said Dzokaya. "But there must be a source. There *must* be."

"A meigysial storm could have any number of sources," said Kyf. "From natural ley line changes to a rogue magister getting an experiment wrong."

"Could be anythin'."

"I *have* thought of something," Pel said, his hand grasping his stubble, "but I'm not sure it's sound."

"I will take any hypothesis," Dzokaya said.

"Could it be a shid?"

Toya gasped as Kyf crossed his arms and leaned back in his chair in contemplation. A silence fell upon the room.

Longing to break it, Dzokaya spoke.

"The thought had crossed my mind, but I have never encountered one," she said.

"They *are* an ancient threat," said Kyf.

"Have any appeared this far west?" Toya inquired.

"If they have, they've been kept a secret."

"Aside from those just outside the Barrier, not that I recall."

Dzokaya looked at Pel confusedly.

"The Barrier Mountains have been a very good meigys shield for Riahla[4]," he explained. "The possibility of a shid passing *through* that barrier...isn't reassuring."

"Is there a barrier to the west?" Dzokaya asked.

"There is. It goes quite far out into the ocean."

"It encircles Riahla."

"But if Dzokaya's able to pass through it, wouldn't that mean a shid could pass through it, too?" asked Toya.

"Oddly enough, it was only meant to block shiden," Pel said. "Has to do with the time it was created."

"Done during the Shiden War, correct?" Kyf said.

"Pretty sure. Can't tell you what year, but yes."

---

4. (REE-ahl-uh) The westernmost nation of Cormoria, Geth Rell being its most well-known oceanfront city, to the south.

"How was it made?" Dzokaya asked.

"That's been lost to time. Some say Qia Mora Herself made it. Others say Serrys and his Order[5] made it. No one knows anymore."

"It just exists, and we're happy it does."

"So, what would that mean if a shid passed through it?"

The two veterans exchanged glances, each expecting the other to answer.

"One of two things," Pel finally said. "Either the barrier is weakened...or the shiden have become more powerful."

"Neither's more desirable than the other," commented Kyf.

Dzokaya leaned her elbows forward on the table and put her head in her hands.

"What am I to do?" she asked herself.

"Slow down, girl," said Kyf. "We don't even know if it *is* a shid or not."

"He's right," Pel added. "It's just a theory."

"Well, you two seem to be *full* of them," Dzokaya huffed, leaning back in her chair with her hands in her lap.

The two men looked at each other, smirking.

"Between wartime, we'd much time to think."

---

5. Serrys and the Ascendants. An order of highly powerful magisters, who some believe sacrificed themselves to create the Riahla Meigys Barrier to protect the country from shiden invasions.

"Between? Has there even *been* a war recently?" asked the girl.

"'Wartime' is probably the wrong word."

"'Conflict' perhaps is better, hm?" Pel suggested.

"Aye."

"Either way, how do you propose we go about finding the source?"

Pel exhaled hard.

"Not sure, to be honest," he said. "I could go around the city asking people. No one would suspect a priest."

"*Former* priest," Kyf corrected.

"In *this* rain?" Toya asked. "Alone?"

"Well, when you put it *that* way—"

"You'd be soaked faster 'an fish in a hurricane."

"Right, but—"

"And what if that *shid*, or whatever, is out there, and it *gets* ya?"

"There *was* a murder this morning," Dzokaya whispered, leaning in toward Pel.

"A *murder?*" exclaimed Toya.

"Yes."

Dzokaya explained the scene she and Pel went to that morning and her findings.

"Well, Pel would know more about that material than I," Kyf said, still leaning back in his chair.

"I'm no magister," Pel replied. "That's why we came here."

Kyf raised an eyebrow.

"What's *here* that'd help you?" he asked.

"That's not what I meant."

"Pel was taking me to the library," Dzokaya interjected. "But the rain was too heavy."

"So, you came here," Kyf finished.

The girl nodded.

"What's at the library?"

"I was hoping I would find something on the Third Force."

Kyf squinted in skepticism.

"You mean that *soul* theory?" he asked. Dzokaya nodded. "You meigys users and your unprovable theories." He sighed. "I can take you there later."

"You're sure?" Pel asked.

"Definitely. If some murderer's on the loose, I bet he bleeds like the rest of us."

Pel frowned slightly.

"That pacifism oath sure looks sour right about now, doesn't it?" Kyf said, smirking.

"I didn't say that," Pel replied.

"No, but your face did," retorted Kyf.

"I'll stay here and pray for you both," said the former priest, mustering up a smile.

"You should come along. Talk to your professor."

"My professor?"

"The one with that conjecture you were telling me about."

"Oh, right."

"The university's not far from the library, you know," said Kyf.

"I'm aware."

"You don't want to go?"

"I do."

"But?"

Pel remained quiet for a moment.

"I can go," he said. "I've been wanting to talk to him for a bit." He turned to Dzokaya. "He might know something that can help you."

Dzokaya smiled at him.

"Good," Kyf replied, sitting up straight and picking up his fork and knife. "We'll leave after breakfast."

The meal resumed in relative gaiety.

4

THE CONJECTURE

A S THE MEN WENT to the den to relax and smoke, Toya asked for Dzokaya's assistance to clean up. The girl had never experienced the daily toil of meal clean up; the house staff was always there to relieve her of that duty.

The men and women she lived with never seemed to rest, in Dzokaya's eyes. No matter what time of day, there were often a handful of maids or butlers doing some chore, saving Dzokaya the mundane joy of making a neat bed or baking a dozen tasty cookies without burning them. The young half-breed was never left in want for something.

Her mother — a beautiful vedzryyf'len chieftess — was reluctant to keep her daughter in these circumstances. The woman came from a tribe that had not seen a human since the Shiden War and lay deep within the dense root jungles that populated one of the smaller inner islands of Mohnaht.

When the slavers came to negotiate a trade, Dzokaya's mother was intrigued by the humans, until then only heard of in stories. But she was no simpleton. The girl's mother had heard of encounters with men called s'tev machen[1] — trader men. They traded with other tribes, who had grown rich with foreign trinkets, but what they traded for was what unsettled this chieftess: they asked for her nynbyrle'len[2] — her hornless people.

She thought it strange to trade boom weapons and shiny metal plates and cups for her tribe members. When she asked the trader men why, they nonchalantly explained to her the customs of other tribes, that they had been trading their hornless and near-hornless members for many years to the men across the ocean, to the north. She asked their leader what her members would be doing in the land of man, but the trader man was hesitant. With a signing of her hand, she was able to extract the answer.

They would be workers in the fields and homes, lovers in the streets and bedchambers. They would be held low in the men's society, as little more than slaves in most instances. They would be playthings and trophies for the aristocracy. They would be beautiful companions to the lonely. They would be servants for royalty. They would

---

1. (seh-TEHV MAHX-ehn)

2. (nihn-BER-leh-lehn) Literally "no horn people."

be farmers on fiber and flour plantations. They would be property to the bankers and loan-givers. They would be barmaids and room cleaners. They would be wombs to rape and faces to beat for the angry. They would be chained to looms in the sweatshops.

And they would be marked with a copper disc in both pointed ears.

Their peoples did this for centuries, and the trader man was stopped before he said much else.

At this, Dzokaya's mother refused to hand the men even a hair from her tribe members' heads. They begged her for something to go back with, so she struck a deal: she would go back with them to Cormoria in exchange for her tribe's complete immunity to their trades. The group of trader men agreed, but not those who succeeded them.

The woman Dzokaya now waved goodbye to had no knowledge of this; neither did the two men she followed. But *she* knew, and her life in Kir Mysch confirmed it.

As Kyf led Dzokaya with a roundell and Pel in a raincoat, the rain had not let up even an ounce; in fact, it appeared to be heavier, though none could say for certain. At a solemn street corner, Kyf and Dzokaya waved at Pel, who walked away and went in the direction of the university.

The university was prestigious in Riahla, but not necessarily in Cormoria whole. And though it was largely looked down upon by Corlia and the Emedyn Rule[3] , some of its professors were of a high caliber. One of these was Professor Rethyfys Hordynfyrt, an authority on Cormorian theology.

Pel made his way to the university quickly so as not to stay too much in the rain; he had an inkling that if he tarried much longer, it would start to bleed through the raincoat.

When he arrived, he took a turn toward the professorial dormitory. The campus was large and spacious, and was quiet as a graveyard, with only the rain pelting the ground as a comrade. The buildings were dated, being out of style even for their construction date with their large, ornate pillars and vines hanging down from long eaves.

The building Pel was going to was one of the oldest on campus; it dated to well before the first century BC[4] . It was the institution's largest structure, and had a large bronze statue of Qia Mora — the Great Mother — standing proudly outside, even as She was doused with angry rain. The windows were unusually tall, even for the time, and had ornate metalwork between the panes of glass, like

---

3. A central Cormorian territory annexed by Corlia during the war between Corlia and Riahla.

4. Before Cormoria. Sometimes abbreviated BCF (Before the Cormorian Formation).

vines trying to pry inside. Around the window and door frames was ancient Pyrmian lettering.

As Pel hastily walked up the steps of the dormitory, he tried to imagine what it would look like if the lettering still retained its glowing power.

Once inside, he shook off the residual rain like a wet dog. He stepped into the atrium and looked down the long, dimly-lit hallways lined with wooden doors. On the walls were paintings of the Great Mother and renditions of moments from the Uch Rynahl[5] ; paladins with fiery swords slaying shiden were common among the works. Gas lamps lit them and the rest of the hall.

His footsteps echoed loudly as he walked to the staircase that led to his destination. At the bottom of the stairs, he looked around and found a registry of all the professors and their apartment locations.

Hordynfyrt's in the C wing, Pel noticed.

Once he found the right direction, he went up the stairs toward that hall.

The hall seemed to go on forever. Door after door lined the left and right, and the lanterns did little to alleviate the illusion. After some time, Pel found the door to Professor Hordynfyrt's apartment.

---

5. (OOX rihn-AHL) The Bible of Qia Mora's worshippers. Literally translated as "Our Story."

He lifted his fist to knock, but hesitated. He was not sure why he did so, but he found it difficult to push through the uneasy and nervous sensations he felt.

Mustering up his resolve, he knocked a few times, stirring up the sound of hard leather soles on wooden floorboards. The person on the other side undid several locks, which clicked out of place, and the door opened.

The man who answered was an older gentleman. He was tall but thin, disguising a hefty appetite, the arms of his shirt rolled up around lanky arms. The doorknob was dwarfed by his long, spidery fingers, which featured large, knobby knuckles. The top buttons of his shirt were undone, and sweat induced from a healthy hearth peppered his hairy chest and brow. His eyebrows were light, matching a pair of equally-light brown eyes and lush, sandy hair streaked with gray. His mustache, however, was bushy and thick, like a hairy caterpillar was taking a nap on his upper lip.

"Can I help you?" the man asked.

Pel was caught off guard by the man's deceptively young voice, but he shook it off and answered.

"Professor Hordynfyrt?" Pel replied.

"Yes?"

"I'm Father Pel. I've come to talk to you about a few things."

The professor's face changed, as if Pel had said something dire.

"Yes. Yes, of course. Come in, Father," Professor Hordynfyrt said, standing aside to let Pel through.

The former priest walked into the apartment, and the professor closed the door behind him.

He was greeted by the smells of the fire and a late breakfast. In front of him was a large rug of the Emedyn Rule style, which sat in front of the fireplace. A couch rested on the wall next to him, and a small card table with two chairs sat over between two long windows. To his left was an entryway into the kitchen.

The room was very warm, and Pel instinctively removed his coat to relieve himself of it. He placed it on the coat stand to the side and stepped further into the room. He could see the kitchen made its way into the bedroom, whose door was slightly ajar.

"May I get something for you, Father?" asked the professor.

"Tea, please."

"Black?"

"Red."

"Yes, Father," Hordynfyrt said, bowing slightly in respect.

He walked to the kitchen to fetch a kettle and some tea, and within a short time, he came back out with the desired material. Pel was still standing on the rug.

"Please, Father," Hordynfyrt said, placing the tea tray on the table. "Come sit. I would hate for a member of the clergy to be uncomfortable."

Pel smirked.

"I'm afraid uncomfortable's my usual state these days," he said.

He pulled out one of the chairs and sat down at the table, both feet on the floor. The professor sat down on the opposite chair, his knees bent up slightly from his long, spidery legs.

"So, Father. What can I do for you?"

"I'm here about a certain article in the paper."

The professor sighed and clenched his fists.

"The Riahla Register?" he asked.

"That one. Yes," replied Pel.

"Hmph! Those people are faster to lie than whores."

Pel frowned in confusion.

"I beg your pardon?" he said.

"The article in the paper was *not* what my conjecture was of," replied the professor with a certain annoyance in his voice.

"I don't understand."

Hordynfyrt sighed.

"I will show you," he said, standing up and walking into a side room.

He returned shortly with a few papers in his hand. He handed them to Pel.

"'Potential Reinterpretations of the Relationship Between the Great Mother and the Shadow Mistress'," Pel read aloud. He looked at Hordynfyrt. "You were attempting to see if They were more than friends? Lovers?"

"Not exactly," the professor said. "It was just *one* possible reinterpretation I listed. The one I wound up settling on — which is *in* the conjecture — is that They were *sisters.*"

"Sisters?" Hordynfyrt nodded. Pel's eyebrows raised. "That can change things. If the Corlian Church gets a hold of this, this...could make you some enemies."

"I am aware. I have already almost been expelled from this university for the Register's false reporting."

"You showed this to your superiors, I assume."

"My colleagues, yes. I was cleared of any wrongdoing...to the point where they are writing to the Register as we speak."

"They wish the article removed?"

"Revised."

"Why not remove it entirely?"

"When has the removal of information ever been benevolent?"

Pel looked back at the papers and flipped through them; there were eight.

"If you don't mind," Pel said, "I'd like to read this."

"By all means," replied the professor. "But I do not think they will survive the storm," he said, gesturing to the window.

Pel smiled.

"Well, I've some tea, here. A warm hearth. I'll read them here. That is, if you don't mind."

"Mind? It would be a pleasure to get some input from someone of a Riahlish Order."

Pel chuckled.

"I'll try not to be long," he said.

"Please, Father," said Hordynfyrt, "take your time. I have nowhere to be."

The two men smiled at each other, and Professor Hordynfyrt walked away, back into the kitchen. Pel placed the papers down on the table, poured himself some tea, and got to reading.

The professor had put forth that the Great Mother of Cormoria and the Shadow Mistress of Mohnaht were either close friends, sisters, lovers, or comrades-in-arms. This reasoning was due to the word "gethyna," meaning sister, being used to refer to each other in various contexts.

Some soldiers during the time of the Uch Rynahl's writing would call each other "geth," meaning brother, if they fought multiple battles with the same men or were even of the same battalion. However, this was not a very common occurrence; in fact, most soldiers who called each other "geth" were somehow related by blood. Female soldiers, though they existed, were exceedingly rare as to be relatively unheard of. However, though modern usage of the term "gethyna" to refer to a female comrade-in-arms is as common as "geth," there are no references to any female soldiers in the Uch Rynahl, so there is no reference point to go by.

With regards to being close friends, the word is similar to "gethyczra," which means a close female friend. It has also been used to indicate a female significant other before marriage, but not a betrothed. The word "gethyna" is often used as a modern replacement for this word by mortals, but would be unlikely to be used by the Ladies Themselves since it is believed they spoke First Pyrmian. It was They, after all, who brought language to the Coren, who then later developed their own dialects.

Coming to the instance of being lovers is tricky, since "gethyna" could be used for a female lover. However, the proper word is "par'bela," but a couple who often saw each other could use the word "geth" and "gethyna," although it would be in a slang form. It is unknown if the Ladies used much slang, if at all. They use no slang in the Uch Rynahl, but it is there, which is why this possibility remains among fringe scholars as They are believed to have authored most of it. Professor Hordynfyrt decided this to be unlikely, since — while They are credited with its creation — when They speak, there is no slang used.

Because of the above, reasoned the professor, it is most likely that when the Ladies refer to each other by "gethyna," it is in its truest form, that being sisters.

Pel put down the papers and sat with his arms folded in contemplation. After a moment, he stood up and walked to the kitchen with the conjecture in hand, where Professor Hordynfyrt sat sipping tea and reading a newspaper. The professor looked up and put the newspaper down.

"Well?" Hordynfyrt said.

"I had my suspicions," Pel said, placing the thesis down on the kitchen table. "But it makes sense to me." Hordynfyrt sighed in relief. "However, the Church of Corlia might not like this."

"Few will."

"Perhaps a small church on the Northern Plains."

"Few *official* orders outside Riahla will accept it."

"Possibly. It would certainly change many orders *here*. But you can take ever visiting Corlia off your Mother's Day list[6]."

The professor sighed.

"What do I do, Father?" he said.

"You said the university's kept you here, correct?"

"Yes."

"So, you still have your position here?"

---

6. The equivalent of a bucket list. Mother's Day is the day on which a person dies, when one meets the Mother Qia Mora in Her solar Heaven.

"Yes, Father."

Pel shrugged.

"I say put it behind you," he said. "If you haven't lost your professorship, there shouldn't be anything to worry about."

"But my reputation."

"What of it?" Pel paused. "Who knows your work? How good it is?" Pel asked.

"Many people. I would hardly know with whom to start."

"Has this conjecture changed that? In a bad way?"

"Not at all! Quite the contrary, actually."

"Then who gives a damn about what others think? The ones who matter think more of you, and those who don't haven't changed. As merchants say, it's an overall profit."

Professor Hordynfyrt nodded slightly, then more vigorously.

"You are right, Father," he said, standing up and taking the papers into his hands. "Thank you."

Pel smiled.

"What're you to do with that, then?" he asked, pointing to the papers.

"I think I will submit it to the Church," the professor said, spirits lifted.

"I'd put in a good word for you, but—"

"I am not sure there is a need for that," Hordynfyrt interrupted. "My colleagues' recommendations should be enough for them."

"Then good luck," Pel said, stretching out a hand.

The two men shook hands firmly.

"You would be a fine paladin, Father," the professor said.

"I'm not so sure of that."

"You should be one. I think you would do some good."

Pel chuckled.

"I appreciate that," he said. "I have another thing to ask."

"Go ahead."

"What do you know of the Third Force?"

"I am afraid I know little. It is not theology, but magistry that you are looking for. I am sorry to say, we have no magistry faculty."

"I see."

"I suggest going to the library nearby."

Pel smiled.

"Thank you," he said, and paused. "I'd best be going." He turned for the door.

"Are you sure you wouldn't want to stay here and wait out the rain?"

"Oh, I don't think it'll end anytime soon."

Hordynfyrt frowned in confusion.

"You do not think it will pass?" he asked.

"Not naturally."

"I would like to hear your conjecture on *that*."

Pel smiled.

"Perhaps another day, Professor. When I have fewer worries on my mind."

Pel took his coat and opened the door.

"Goodbye, Professor," he said. "It's been enlightening."

"Thank you, as well, Father."

The two men waved at each other, and Pel stepped out into the hall. He put on his raincoat and walked away. As he made his way down the stairs of the lobby, he noticed a man in a raincoat and hat walk up the opposite flight. He thought it strange that the man would continue wearing a hat indoors, but he shrugged it off and stepped outside.

With his curiosity satisfied, Pel smirked at the encounter and started for the library.

5

IT IS REAL

THE WIND KICKED UP as Pel walked hastily to the library. He did not have much distance to cover, but the dismal weather made it feel like miles.

As he rounded a corner in the direction of the library, a sudden melancholy fell over him, mingled with an intense fear and anger. He could not control it, and it consumed him. He had the idea to turn and go back to the tavern, and as he turned, a horror unlike any other loomed over him.

Furled in a huge cloud of black and white smoke, a large, eyeless maw covered in scaly scabs and boils was open, showing its hundreds of sharp teeth. Tendrils meekly reached out for Pel as it whispered to him in a language he did not know, but understood perfectly as if he had spoken it since birth. It spoke his name in a chilling, deep voice that echoed in the streets and Pel's mind.

The sight struck Pel from these negative emotions, and he took the Great Mother's name in vain. He ran as quickly as he could from the horror; it followed him with the sound of a snarling steam engine. He thought he could hear chains clanging as it chased him.

Pel made the Sign of the Mother and prayed to Her as he ran.

"O, Mother, protect me from evil which seeks to take me from Your loving embrace."

As if Qia Mora had bestowed upon Pel a blessing, he found his steps suddenly lighter and faster than before as he kept ahead of the ungodly beast that reached for his heels.

After a frightful eternity, he came in sight of the library, its huge facade looming over a small square. Pel was filled with a newfound resolve, and soon he reached the library's gigantic doors. He looked behind himself and saw the horrific cloud and maw speeding toward him. With all his might, he pushed open a smaller door set within the larger and slammed it shut with more strength than he thought he had.

The librarian shushed him as he stood pushing against the door with open hands and arms outstretched, panting. His eyes nearly bulged out of his head; he could not blink for fear of not seeing the thing coming after him so he could move out of its grasp.

Noticing the several locks on the door, Pel immediately engaged them and turned around, leaning his back against the door.

The bewildered priest looked around the huge room lined with books and tables, and walked swiftly away, toward the front desk.

On either side of the central information desk were tables for reading and doing work. Beyond those, lining the unusually-high walls, were bookcases upon bookcases that went up to the illustriously-painted ceiling. More bookcases jutted out from the walls perpendicularly and had iron scaffolding encircling them. In a brief glance, Pel made out four levels of books above him.

"Excuse me," Pel managed to muster. "Have you seen a young girl and a tall man come in here recently?"

"A young *vedzryyf'len* girl?" the middle-aged woman asked.

"Yes," he nodded.

"They headed toward the Meigys Section. Make a left through there," she said, pointing to the main hall, "and go up the stairs. You won't miss it."

"Thank you," Pel said, still panting.

"Excuse me, but...are you alright?" the librarian asked. "You look as if you've seen a specter or something."

"You could say that," he said before walking away.

Did he see a specter, or was it something else? It did not speak any language he recognized, nor did it look like a specter. Could it have been a shid? Pel thought it unlikely, but he had no idea what a shid looked like. He had heard shiden could take any form they wished, but he figured they tended to seduce people, not try to chase them through the streets to eat them.

He walked confused and still scared through the library. But something about the place was slowly bringing peace to him; it was bringing him comfort. It was as if he were in a cathedral of great holiness, something he had felt before in his early years as a priest-in-training.

The library was fairly empty — as it would in such a storm. The halls were great and made of a white marble and granite. The ceilings were high, and large paintings lined the walls. Pel even saw a tapestry or two — one of which he had only read about in his priestly studies — but he paid no mind to them.

He eventually made it to the Meigys Section and started searching for Kyf and Dzokaya; it did not take long. Pel found them sitting together with a stack of tomes between them at a far table. The former priest hastily walked over to them.

The couple heard his footsteps as he managed closer, and they looked up from their material to see a panicked, pale Pel speeding his way toward them. Kyf placed his hands flat on the table and stood up.

"Pel, my friend," Kyf said. "What's gotten to you? Are you sick?"

"Nearly," Pel replied.

"Sit, man. I haven't anything to drink, unfortunately."

"That's alright," the former priest said, sitting down across from the other two. "I'm not sure I could stomach it after what I just saw."

"I assume it is the reason you look as you do," Dzokaya said, sounding somewhat concerned.

Pel nodded vigorously.

"It is." He looked around himself before speaking. "I met a *shid*," he whispered.

"You *what?*" Kyf exclaimed.

The others shushed him.

"I swear it was," Pel pleaded.

He then described what he had seen in all its detail. Dzokaya and Kyf sat dumbfounded. Kyf knew Pel was not lying, but Dzokaya was less certain; he was a human, after all, and humans were wont to fib.

"Are you sure that is what you saw?" Dzokaya asked, squinting in skepticism.

"Absolutely," replied Pel.

"Could it have been a trick of the light? Or a magisterial illusion?"

"That doesn't sound to *me* like some magister playing a practical joke," Kyf retorted.

"I doubt his sight."

"Why's that?"

Dzokaya sat quietly with a face that simply said she was reluctant to divulge her reasoning.

"Look at him," said Kyf, gesturing to his friend. "Does he look like he's jesting? Or telling a tale?"

Pel's breathing had slowed down slightly, and the color was just starting to return to his face.

The girl pressed her lips together tightly.

"I suppose not," she relented.

"By the Mother, a shid's what I saw. Like nothing of this world."

Dzokaya sighed, knowing she would have more work ahead of her.

"I suppose I could look through some more textbooks to find your shid—"

"I think *I'd* be better suited for that. *I'm* the one who saw it."

Dzokaya's face shifted into an acquiescent countenance.

"Have you found anything useful while I was gone?" Pel asked.

"A little," she said. "I have found a handful of treatises on the Three Forces."

"Then why do you look like you haven't found a damned thing?"

"Because they all say the same thing. That the Third Force is *beyond* the corporeal."

"Meaning?" asked Kyf.

"Meaning that it's not physically detectable," Pel explained.

"There is no way to prove or disprove its existence. Which is what I figured."

"Then why'd you come here in the first place if you knew what you'd find?" Kyf asked.

Dzokaya closed the book in front of her and leaned into the middle of the table.

"Vedzryyf'len have the ability to *see* meigys," she whispered. "When we die, our meigys goes into the aether. That man we saw still retained his meigys."

The three sat silent for a moment, as if each were waiting for the other to finish the thought.

"I think he was drained of his Third Force," the half-breed finally said.

"Ridiculous!" Kyf ejaculated.

The others shushed him.

"Ridiculous," Kyf whispered. "That would mean shiden can go undetected. And they don't."

"As far as *we* know," Pel said. "But that would also mean they can go through the Barrier. All it'd need to do is somehow convert meigys into the Third Force and pass right through."

Kyf raised an eyebrow.

"*That's* an explanation," he said in disbelief and frustration.

"If the Barrier surrounding Riahla is based off the Two Force Principle, then it is very likely a shid with access to the *Third* Force could simply cross it without any issue," said the girl.

The three sat wide-eyed at the revelation.

The Three Forces Theory had long gone out of favor. Centuries before the Cormorian Formation, it was widely accepted there were three Forces: the Corporeal Force, the Bridging Force, and the Aethereal Force. However, as test after test failed to prove the existence of the Aethereal Force, the theory was eventually dropped by magisters and scholars alike; by the first century of the Cormorian Formation, texts on the Three Forces Theory were shelved as ancient pseudoscience.

"Why now, though?" Pel said to himself.

"What do you mean?"

"All shiden being equal — that is, they're all *shiden* — why've they not figured this out yet? I mean, the Barrier's been up for *how many* centuries, and they just *now* start to appear?" Pel sat up straight and crossed his arms. "Something doesn't smell right."

"Can you *summon* a shid?" Dzokaya asked.

"Don't know, love. Never tried."

"Well, we're not going to start."

"You've got what you came for, girl?"

"I have got as much as I *will* get."

"Then we should be off," Kyf said, standing up.

Pel and Dzokaya agreed, and they stood up from the table.

"I just have to put these back," said the girl, grabbing the stack of tomes.

"Leave 'em," said Kyf, putting his arm out in front of her. "It'll give that librarian something to do."

Dzokaya looked at Pel, as if waiting for his approval, which took the form of a lazy shrug. She placed the stack on the table, and they began to walk out of the section.

As the trio exited, their footfalls echoing in the empty halls, they saw a man in a raincoat walking toward them, holding a hat by its brim. The four saw each other, and while the men did not recognize each other, the other called to the half-breed.

"Dzokaya?" said the man.

She turned and eyed him.

He was nearly as tall as Kyf, though twice as girthy. His raincoat was open, which let an eye view his vest and gold watch chain that linked across it. His shoes were wet and shone from the wall lamps. His thin mustache hung like a high chandelier over his mouth, and his salt-and-pepper mutton chops framed a mildly-wrinkled face.

"Sir Dumentyn!" Dzokaya said.

"What are *you* doing here?" he asked.

"I could ask the same of you," the girl replied. "I have not known you to be studious."

There was a moment of silence as Sir Dumentyn looked at Pel and Kyf, and thought about his reply.

"I am...looking...for a book," Sir Dumentyn answered.

"Well, here's a great place to find one," said Kyf, smirking at his own comment.

"Yes, well...what, uh, what...what are *you* doing here? I thought you were dead."

"No. I was not with my parents when they...died."

"I—I...I am glad." There was a moment of thick silence. "Well, you should be off, now. You must have...matters to attend to."

"I do."

"Take care!" said Sir Dumentyn as he walked away, waving his hat in the air as a goodbye.

The three looked at each other.

"Well, *he* was odd," Kyf said.

"Indeed," Pel added. "The man seemed...unnerved, I'd say."

Dzokaya nodded.

"We should make haste," she said to the men.

"Yes, we should," Pel replied.

The group rushed down the lengthy marble staircase, quickly into the main hall. Pel and Kyf waved farewell to the librarian.

"There's a bunch of books in the Meigys Section that need tending," said Kyf in a raised tone.

The librarian scowled slightly at him.

Pel went to undo the locks he had put on, but noticed they were undone. He shrugged; the librarian must have taken them off. He opened the door, the sound of heavy rain greeting them as they walked out.

As the triplet was descending the steps to the library, Dzokaya stopped for a moment at the bottom, the two men walking past her. Kyf and Pel stopped, and turned around to see the half-breed girl standing in the rain looking at the wet cobblestones.

"Dzokaya?" Pel said.

Suddenly, from atop the steps of the library, Pel bore witness to the same abomination that had nearly gotten him. His and Kyf's eyes nearly shot out of their skulls at the sight.

"Dzokaya!" Pel shouted as he ran after her.

The closer the man got to her, the closer the beast got. He was not sure if he would make it, but he did. The former priest tugged on Dzokaya, but she would not budge. Pel looked over her to see the vile entity pull back its tendrils and then thrust them at her. As if imbued with supernatural speed, Pel grabbed the girl by her arms and threw her far behind him onto the cobblestones. When she made contact with the ground, she seemed to break out of her trance and looked at her savior.

At that moment, as Pel stood before Kyf and Dzokaya, several of the ungodly creature's tendrils pierced the priest.

"Pel!" shouted Kyf.

As he collapsed into a deep puddle, the creature removed its tendrils and moved after the other two. Kyf rushed to Dzokaya's aid and lifted her up.

"Run!" he commanded.

Unsure of what to make of the situation, Dzokaya looked at Pel, then at the monster. At that moment, she could not worry about Pel nor what would become of him. She decided to run for her life.

A white owl followed silently above.

6

— · —

SKIRMISH

DZOKAYA AND KYF RAN as the rain pelted their faces. Lightning flashed, casting momentary shadows of the city around them. With Kyf's hand in her grasp, Dzokaya followed him as best she could, all the while the voracious fiend followed with rampant hunger — for what, the young half-breed knew not. Their steps fell heavy on the wet cobblestone, and Dzokaya nearly lost her footing as the couple rounded several corners in an effort to evade the vile creature.

No, it was not just a creature; it was the embodiment of a hungering evil, with a lust for devouring life, that which only mortals cherished and understood; it was a shid. And yet, this monstrosity seemed attracted to it like a bee to nectar. Never had Dzokaya witnessed such a disgusting and terrifying thing as to stricken her with sheer horror and cause her to recoil at its guise.

After a heart-pounding perpetuity, Dzokaya found herself led back to Kyf's home.

"Get inside!" the man commanded.

She obeyed and rushed inside as Kyf slammed the door behind them. He engaged the lock — a sturdy deadbolt — and unholstered his pistol, which he hoped would work. He had never fought a shid before, nor had he ever thought he would.

The beast flew at the house and crashed against its stone walls with a thunderous boom. Kyf was pushed away from the door, but swiftly moved back to his former position against it. Again, the fiend flew into the house and was again repelled, a flash of golden light was barely hidden by the curtains.

Meanwhile, Dzokaya had run up the stairs to the bathroom. Lying on the floor was her sword — her mother's weapon, which had been passed down from her mother and her mother's mother. It seemed ancient to the girl; it was a deep crescent blade, with a handle that bent from the middle of the spine along the back. It was a strange item, black as the darkest night, yet it reflected even the most dim sunlight. One of the flats of the blade was uneven and jagged, like it was forged from the bark of some absurd tree.

Dzokaya unsheathed the blade and brought it downstairs. Kyf managed to hold the door closed, but each successive thrust into the abode the shid made, the more he felt his strength leave him. Toya stood peaking behind the kitchen door.

"Open the door!" Dzokaya shouted.

"You're mad, girl! You'll die!"

"I can repel it!"

As the abomination made another lunge, Kyf unlatched the door. The impact of the beast flung open the door and threw Kyf into the den, a flash of golden light briefly making itself known.

Dzokaya rushed out into the rain, sword in hand.

Before her rested the terrible shid, pustule-ridden maw agape and drooling in anticipation of its potential meal. The two stood against each other as if they were in a Midland Plains duel. Dzokaya was petrified, her hands shaking in the chilling rain. But she knew she had to fell the creature.

After a nerve-racking stand-off, the shid rushed at the half-breed. Dzokaya quickly slid her hand along the jagged flat of her blade and let loose a bolt of dark energy, striking her foe in its snout. It stopped suddenly, and Dzokaya let fly another bolt in the same manner. The bolt struck the beast, carving a chunk of black, oozing flesh from its lip and shattering teeth. The monster recoiled in pain, its many tendrils flailing in angered frustration.

Meanwhile, Kyf lifted himself off the floor. Through the window, he witnessed Dzokaya throw a bolt of energy at her enemy, eliciting the demonic roar of the shid. He tried to think quickly of how best to protect her. He had a gun, but would it work? Then, he eyed the carved Mother's Sword above the entryway. He had to act quickly, and indeed, he did. He rushed to grab the Sword and ventured outside into the downpour.

And it was not a moment too late.

Kyf's appearance distracted Dzokaya only momentarily, but it was enough for the shid to quickly disarm the girl with one of its tendrils, slapping the blade from her hand and embedding it into a stud of the house. With pistol in hand, Kyf lifted up the Sword in front of himself and took aim at the monster. It unleashed a horrific cry and lunged at the man. He fired at it, each shot landing true. Yet the lead bullets did naught against the unholy fiend.

Now it loomed over Kyf and Dzokaya, drooling a black sludge that reeked of dead, decaying flesh. Kyf stood in front of the girl and, realizing he was out of shots, held high the Mother's Sword in what he thought was a vain act. The shid opened its stinking, slimy jaws and clamped down on the pair. However, its teeth were halted by the sudden creation of a golden dome over its prey. It tried again to eat them, but it failed, the golden dome appearing again before its bite.

Kyf still held the wooden Sword tightly in his hands, drenched in rain as he was. The shid tried to fling it out of his grasp, but the dome again prevented its move. The creature grew frustrated and flailed all its limbs at the man, and all were stopped by the same golden dome.

Suddenly, a man's voice yelled from the darkness at the shid in some language neither Kyf nor Dzokaya recognized. They looked to see where the voice came from, but they only saw the silhouette of a man. The beast growled. Kyf turned and watched the creature. After a brief flash of lightning and a moment of what seemed like hesitation, it flew at the man. Their forms combined, and they both disappeared into the shadows.

Kyf stood shaking from adrenaline, and Dzokaya stood crouched, cowering behind him. They looked at each other, then back at the spot where the man was. He turned and faced the holy symbol in that direction. After a few moments, when nothing seemed to come at him, Kyf lowered the Sword and fell to his knees.

"Qia Mora," he whispered loudly. "Thank You."

He kissed the Sword in his hands as thanks for its aid.

"What was that?" Toya exclaimed, blanket in hand.

Dzokaya and Kyf were silent.

"Where's Pel?" the woman asked.

Kyf stood up and gathered Dzokaya in his arms. She was still shaking in fear, but Kyf thought she may be getting ill.

"Come on," he said to her.

He led the shivering girl toward the door. She grabbed her sword and, bracing her foot against the wall, pulled it out. They went inside.

"What happened?"

"Take her upstairs," Kyf said, guiding the girl into his wife's arms.

He placed the Mother's Sword back into its mount and closed the door, locking it.

"I don't understand. What's goin' on?"

Suddenly, Dzokaya fainted, shivering through unconsciousness.

"Take her to Liora's room," Kyf commanded. "Dry her off and bundle her up."

Kyf grabbed the girl and hoisted her up into his arms.

"Will ye *please* tell me what's goin' on?" Toya asked as Kyf started up the stairs.

"A shid," he said as he climbed.

"A *what?*" his wife said, following swiftly behind.

"A shid. A *vile* thing, it is."

"What do we do? Where's Pel?"

Kyf opened the door to his daughter's bedroom and walked inside. He looked back at his wife with stern sadness in his eyes.

"He's dead," he said flatly.

Toya could hardly fathom the statement. She had known the priest for as long as she had known her husband; she had expected the three of them to die old and happy. But now, that dream vanished before her. Tears welled up in her pretty eyes as she stood in the doorway to her daughter's room and watched Kyf place Dzokaya on a chair.

The man turned to his wife.

"I'll leave the undressing to you," he said.

She nodded, trying not to burst out into sorrowful wails, and moved to strip Dzokaya. Kyf pulled the door closed behind him and stood silent for a moment, listening to the dripping of his clothes hit the floorboards.

He tried to focus on it, the swift drip-drip that only occurred when a fabric was sufficiently soaked. The scene of his friend's death — his murder — played in his mind. Over and over, he watched, with heart-wrenching sadness, his friend get pierced by some baleful abomination. Slow tears mingled with the water that dripped down his face. He sighed deeply and moved to go down to the main room.

Kyf had always kept two holy books.

The first was *the* holy book: the Uch Rynahl. It was the story of his people; how they came to the continent that was once Pyrmia; how they settled and flourished in this new land; of how Qia Mora — the Great Mother — guided them and saw fit their lives and ruled them; of the first Shiden Wars. It was a book of history and prayer, a book that any self-respecting Moran kept close and dear in his home.

The other was less well known, hidden — unmarked — among some old books on a small bookshelf. It was equally as old — something that looked to be passed down through generations — and he carried it with him throughout his career as a Riahlish soldier. He grabbed this one and opened it.

Inside was a sealed flask with the army's insignia. Kyf took it out and placed the book down. He gazed reluctantly at the flask. It had served him well during difficult times: when he had to put down a vedzryyf'len rebellion; when he was instructed to fire upon a settlement of "unwanted" Gek'reken; when a myriad of things occurred that he was instructed to do simply because it was the order of a superior.

As he opened the flask, he was reminded of the oath he and Pel made when they left the military, toasting with matching flasks.

"To protect those who cannot protect themselves," echoed in his mind, his eyes moist from tears.

He held high the flask and toasted to his comrade. He took a drink, grimacing at the strong alcohol that burned its way down his throat like lava. He was not used to such strong drink.

The veteran sat in silent contemplation for a long time until there was a knock on the door.

Strange, Kyf thought, *no one's been out in this weather.*

Putting the flask back into its hideaway, he went to the door and opened it. He stood dumbfounded and blinked many times to understand what was before him.

It was Pel!

His clothes were torn, and holes were where he had been pierced. But instead of blood and bare muscle, there was scarred skin. In his eyes was a strange brightness.

"Pel!"

Kyf put his hand out, which the other took, and they pulled each other in for a hug. They stood in each other's arms for a few moments. Then, they let go.

"Come in, friend."

Kyf closed the door behind him. Then, he noticed something in Pel's hand.

"Is that—" Kyf started to say.

Pel turned and held up a sword. It was plain; a long, rectangular guard sat butted up against the locket of a long scabbard, which was worn and aged. The sword's grip was longer than the crossguard, worn more than the scabbard, and terminated in a featureless, circular pommel.

"It is," Pel said.

"But how?"

"First, how about we get out of these wet clothes?"

"You can tell me while we undress," Kyf said.

"Alright," said Pel as he put the sword down and took off his coat.

———◆———

Meanwhile, Toya had undressed Dzokaya and put her in her daughter's bed. She had put the girl's sword and clothes on a desk in the meantime. The woman covered her in several quilts as she shivered violently.

"Easy there," Toya said in a motherly tone. "Ye alright."

Toya wondered what the shid was like. It was clearly very strong. But what was that light that appeared? Was that the Great Mother? Was *She* protecting them?

"Mother, help us," she said, making the Sign of the Mother.

She knelt next to the bed for a while, praying.

———◆———

The fireplace crackled vibrantly as the former priest stood before it, warming his hands. Kyf sat in his underwear as the cushioned chair soaked up the rain dripping off him. He was grasping his chin in thought.

"That's quite the story," he said. "That light in your eyes," he paused. "Is that from Her?"

"It is," Pel replied. "Is it noticeable?"

"A bit."

Pel stood over the fire, leaning on the mantle.

"It was something...to see Her," he said.

"I bet it was. And She gave you a gift."

"Paladinhood."

"A second chance."

"I'm not sure I deserve one."

"If She gave you one, you most certainly deserve it," Kyf said, releasing his chin. "Pel," he said, standing, "this is the chance we need. To rid ourselves of this shid."

"Where is it?" Pel asked.

Kyf frowned.

"I don't know," he said. "It disappeared."

"Dzokaya's safe?"

"I assure you. You can check upstairs if you'd like."

"I'd rather get into some dry clothes," Pel smiled.

"Hmph," Kyf smirked. "Come with me."

The two men walked to a back room. It was of a modest size, and fit a small bed and some furniture comfortably. Kyf opened up a drawer, pulled out some clothes, and handed them to Pel.

"More of your brother's?"

"Aye."

Pel took the clothes.

"I hope he won't mind my wearing them."

"He won't," Kyf said before he started to walk out.

"Why didn't you have me get dressed in here before?"

Kyf's eyebrow raised.

"I just didn't think of it, I guess," he said.

"Is *that* right?"

"Well, you caught me so off-guard, I hardly knew what to do. It's not very often we get sudden visitors. And in *this* weather?"

The two men smiled at each other. Kyf walked out and closed the door behind him.

It was such a strange situation, to see your friend murdered and comeback to life all in the same day. And brought back by the Great Mother Herself, no less. Kyf exhaled hard and ran a hand through his hair.

He went up to his bedroom and got dressed into some dry clothes. As he walked out of the room, he noticed Toya coming out of their daughter's room. He walked over to her.

"How is she?" he asked.

"Shiverin' cold," replied Toya. "But she's bundled up nicely."

"Good," Kyf said, putting an arm around her. "I've got a guest downstairs."

"Another one?"

The couple walked down to the den. Pel was sitting in a chair watching the fire dance. Toya turned to her husband.

"I thought ya said he was dead," she said.

"Qia Mora brought him back," Kyf said as they went over to him.

"Is that true?"

Pel smiled.

"It is," he said. "Tall tale as it may be, She indeed gave me a second chance."

As the loving couple went to sit with Pel, the faint, golden light in Pel's eyes became apparent to her. She sat down in another chair and stared at him.

"Yer eyes," she said, almost in a whisper. "Yer a paladin?"

"It would seem so," replied Pel.

Toya gasped.

"A paladin?" she said. "In Riahla? Never thought I'd see the day."

"As did we all," Kyf said, sitting next to his wife. "Although, while Pel's new strength is a boon, how do we go about ridding ourselves of this evil?"

Pel sat back in his seat and folded his arms.

"Well, you said it disappeared," said the newly-made paladin.

"Fled, to be more precise," said Kyf.

"Fled?"

"Yes. A man called to it, and it followed him."

"What did he say?"

"Don't know. It was a language I've never heard. But that shid understood clearly."

"What did he look like?"

"I couldn't get a good sight on him. It was too dark."

"Perhaps Dzokaya saw him."

"She may've."

"Well, ye'll have to wait till she's able," Toya interjected. "She's had a terrible fright. She has ta rest."

"That's wise. She should be strong if we're to take it on again."

"Aye. The thing could be gathering its strength."

"How long do you think she'll be out?" asked the newly-made paladin.

"Could be a while," Toya replied. "She was shiverin' cold, but much more than just cold. The excitement must've gotten ta her."

"Excitement. Fright. If that's the case, the girl's too frail to fight a shid," said Kyf.

"Perhaps," said Pel. "But now that she's come face to face with it, perhaps she could better protect herself against it."

"Possibly," Kyf grumbled.

"She's better than nothing."

"She could be a liability."

"Geth!" said Toya. "She's not even awake yet, let alone recovered." She paused. "Make the decision when it's pertinent ta."

"Fair enough," Kyf said.

"What do we do until then?" asked Pel. "It's too dangerous to go back to the library to read upon shiden warfare."

"We wait," said Kyf, standing up. "I've got to reload my pistol." He started over toward the stairs.

"Did it do anything?"

Kyf stopped, silent.

"No," he finally said. "But it's better than nothing. Especially if that man comes around. The two are bound somehow."

"I wonder if the Uch Rynahl has anything about it."

"I've got one over there," Kyf said, pointing to a large bookcase near the hearth. "Read what you like. I need something more tangible."

Kyf walked up the stairs as Pel went to retrieve the holy book.

7

REVELATIONS

KYF WALKED INTO HIS second floor workshop and closed the door. He took out his pistol and sat at the workbench, tossing down the weapon with a thud. It was his old service weapon: a break-action seven-shot. He had relied on it before, but he had not used it in years aside from regular practice. Today was the first time he used it in aggression, albeit in self-defence.

He looked at it like it was an old friend he had not seen in a longtime. He flipped it over in his hands, looking for any mark the shid may have made on it. Its bluing was fading, slowly rubbed away by its holster, and small, insignificant scratches were scattered on the barrel and cylinder, marks of a time Kyf remembered with mixed emotions.

He unlocked the frame and hinged it forward, pulling up the extractor and emptying the cylinder, the spent shells scattering across the bench. Then, he started to clean it.

This was a ritual he had developed since being in the army. But this time was different. It was not the usual maintenance he would do to his weapon, no. This was an effort to calm himself and rationalize what had just transpired. The last time he did this, he had taken part in a horrendous act.

A shid in Riahla, he thought. *Mother, help us.*

Kyf breathed deeply as the visage of the shid floated across his mind's eye. A shiver ran up his spine, and he quickly snapped his gaze around himself, as if looking for an unseen threat.

"Easy, Sergeant," he said to himself.

He took another deep breath and tried to drop his shoulders. The pistol stared back at him like a confused child watching its father deal with something greater than them both. Kyf shook and grabbed the rag he was using, his hands shaking.

Why was he having so much trouble with this...*thing?*

Kyf searched his mind for reasons, but all he could find was fear — deep, impenetrable fear. Indeed, the man had faced death once before, and yet he was not so afraid as he was now. Of course, the two incidents were wildly different: one was instigated by a vedzryyf'len, while the other was of a completely alien agent that could have destroyed his very being.

Yet, he was alive.

He was not a particularly religious man, seeing Moranism as something too aethereal to grasp. But now, Kyf was made a bystander by the very thing he thought beyond him. The Sword protected him; *the Mother* protected him. Had he not witnessed it himself, he would have thought it a thing of the imagination, a trick of a magister, or some other explicable phenomenon.

Kyf dropped his pistol on the bench and put his head in his hands, still shaking; whether it was from the adrenaline or fear — or the holy revelation before him — he knew not.

He looked at the pistol.

Nothing, he thought. *It did nothing.*

The former soldier stared at his weapon as an overwhelming sense of impotence washed over him.

———◆———

Toya watched Pel as he read the Uch Rynahl. His eyes raced across the pages as if starvingly devouring the text. The light in his eyes — a faint golden hue — caught her attention once again. Her brow furrowed, and she walked over to him.

"Is there anything I can getcha?" she asked, craning her head to get a better look.

Pel looked up from the book, and Toya's eyes widened slightly.

"No," he said with a smile. "But thank you." He noticed her face and frowned. "Are you alright?"

"They're real," she half-whispered.

"What are?"

"Ya eyes," Toya paused. "I can't get used ta them."

"Likewise. But I consider myself fortunate I have them."

"Is it fortunate that we've need of a paladin?"

Pel frowned.

"Perhaps not," he said.

Toya sat down across from him.

"Only one was out there. If there's one, there's bound to be dozens. *Hundreds*, even."

"Perhaps more," Pel said, pulling the book back up to his face. "After this one, we'll know."

As Pel read the good book, and Toya practiced her embroidery, Kyf walked down the stairs in a slow, tired manner, his heavy footfalls thudding on the hardwood steps. The paladin looked up from his reading and gazed at him.

"You alright, my friend?" Pel asked.

Kyf nodded.

"I am," he said, pausing. "At least...as right as I *could* be."

"Sit, man."

He sat near his wife, who saw there was an oddness about him.

"Sweetheart, ya look ill."

"I feel," Kyf paused in thought. "I'm not sure."

Pel closed the book and placed it on a nearby side table.

"I've seen this before," Pel said.

Toya turned to him.

"Ya have?" she asked. "Where?"

Pel sat silent, knowing full well where that face Kyf had was from. It was a face they both had worn during their later years in the army. They had seen horrible things, acts that few among them seemed to have cared about. But they struck these two men in their hearts — in their souls. Indeed, Gendytha Point played before Pel's imagination like a film faintly superimposed over the sight of Kyf.

The paladin hesitated to bring this up. He leaned forward in interest.

"What did you see, Kyf?" he asked, slowly.

Kyf looked at him with sad and scared eyes, tears coating them in a film that, had he blinked, would surely cascade into a waterfall.

"*Evil*, Pel. Evil the likes of which I've never seen before. Not even at Gendytha."

Indeed, the gravity of what had transpired suddenly hit him and weighed heavy.

"I faced it, Pel."

"You *faced* it? And *lived?*"

With quivering hands, Kyf pointed at the Sword above the doorway.

"Qia Mora...protected us," the man said.

"Mother of Man," whispered the paladin.

He turned to Kyf, who was staring at his shaking hands.

Pel understood, now, that — though Kyf had seen horrors of men — his experience as a soldier failed to prepare him for the horrors of Hell. Indeed, his lack of firm belief prevented Kyf from properly guarding himself against the threat they now faced.

"I...didn't think—"

"No need to think, man," interrupted Pel. "Rest, now ...and pray. Go up to your bedroom and pray. Then sleep. She'll protect you."

Frightened tears streamed down Kyf's face, and Toya held him tight in an effort to comfort him.

Pel frowned.

"Why aren't you like him?" he asked.

"I didn't see it," replied Toya.

Pel wondered, given her own beliefs, if she might have been better off against it than her husband.

After a moment, Toya led her husband to the bedroom, then closed the door. She had never seen him like this before. This wasn't mere fright, but terror.

As she returned to the den, Pel spoke up.

"Is Dzokaya the same?"

Toya shook her head as she sat down.

"No. But she did faint."

Pel crossed his arms and put a thumb to his chin.

"If I have to rely on *one* of them, I'd rather it be her," he said. "*She* has what to use against it. But if she's the same as Kyf," he paused, "then we're in trouble."

Pel and Toya sat quietly for a while as Dzokaya rested above them.

The girl was bundled in heavy quilts, sleeping. She lay quietly and motionless, the only evidence of life the bare rise and fall of the blankets.

And she dreamt.

She was walking with her parents in a bright street, the trio enjoying themselves, laughing. Then, dark smoke rose up around them and stole away her parents, who withered and decayed. Behind them was the man she had seen call the shid, clear as day, with a sinister smile on his face.

She awoke with a start. There was dim light about her, which came from a short candle; it rested on a side table, a small key sitting next to it. Carefully lowering the blankets, she realized she was in small-clothes and quickly pulled the blankets to herself. Her hair was still damp. She looked to her side to find a sleeping Pel slumped in a chair, the Uch Rynahl in his hands.

How? she thought.

But then, in an instant, great joy overtook her, and she threw herself onto him, embracing him tightly. Pel awoke with a snort, then lightly hugged her back.

"Well," he said through a groggy smirk, "I'm glad to see you're also well."

Dzokaya pulled back and looked at him, smiling.

"You died so I could live," she said.

"It seemed the right thing to do at the time."

She hugged him again — tighter this time — then, as she pulled back, she kissed him on the cheek.

"For saving me," she said as she went back into the bed.

Pel was colored surprised. He put his hand to his kissed cheek briefly.

"Thanks," he said. "But I'd rather you regain your strength."

"I think I have."

The paladin patted the girl's hands, which rested on her lap.

"We'll wait till morning."

As Pel closed his eyes, Dzokaya shook him awake.

"I know who he was," she said loudly.

"'He' who? Who's 'he'?"

"That man...with the shid."

Pel steadied himself.

"What man?"

"The man who called the shid. He disappeared with it before I fainted."

Pel attempted to sit comfortably.

"Kyf informed me," he said. "Though, he said he faced it."

Dzokaya straightened her posture and hung her feet off the bed, but under the quilt.

"After you saved me, Kyf brought me here. He barred the door while the shid was trying to get us."

"What did you do?"

"I got my mother's sword and—and faced it."

"You, too?"

"We *both* did. He saved me with Qia Mora's Sword."

Pel thought back to his moment with Kyf earlier, the man's words echoing in the paladin's mind.

"It created a—a barrier that protected us. It could not penetrate it."

"So, what about this man?"

"Sir Dumentyn," she said, marveling at the name.

Pel raised an eyebrow.

"You mean that man from the library?" he asked.

"Yes! He called to it from the dark, and it went to him."

"And they disappeared."

"Yes," Dzokaya said. "But I think I know where they went."

"He's got a favorite haunt?"

"Better. He has a home here."

"In Geth Rell?"

The girl nodded vigorously.

"I guess he's here early," said Pel. "Summer doesn't start for another month."

"If we can find him — ask him questions — we can then discover the whereabouts of the shid."

"We? *I* am going to ask him questions. *You* are going to rest more."

"I will not tell you if you do not take me with you," the girl smirked.

The paladin sighed.

"Fair enough," he said. "Tell me."

"He's on three eighty-four West Sereth Street, between fourth and fifth."

"He's not too far."

The half-breed affirmed eagerly. Pel's brow furrowed.

"Wait. You know where this man is, but you didn't know where the library was?"

"I have never gone far from his home. That tavern was the furthest I had been since then."

Pel's face became acquiescent. Then, he placed the Uch Rynahl on the table with the candle and stood up.

"Thanks for letting me know," he said, smirking.

"Let me get dressed," Dzokaya energetically requested.

"Take your time."

Pel walked out of the room and closed the door. Then, she heard the lock engage. Eyes wide, Dzokaya rushed to the door and tried to open it; it was locked. She looked at the table with the candle and lifted the book. The key was gone.

"Sly devil," she whispered before she sat down on the bed, arms folded.

Meanwhile, Pel made his way down to the den, placed the key on the table in the sitting area, and took up his sword, strapping it to his waist. He donned a kite coat and broad-brimmed hat, and stepped outside, closing the door behind him.

Standing under the overhanging second floor, he looked about himself. Then, he headed in the direction of Sir Dumentyn's home.

Above, a white owl followed silently.

8

---·---

BATTLE OF WILLS

PEL STOOD OUTSIDE AN old home of Geth Rell, further toward the southern shore. It was difficult to make out the features of the building in the dark, though the ornateness and numerous filigrees could be spied with a flash of lightning. He stood looking up at the front door from the bottom of the stoop, rain sliding off the rear brim of his hat like a river. Making the Sign of the Mother, he prayed silently before taking a breath and stepping up.

He grabbed the large knocker and smacked it against the heavy wooden door; an echo rang out from behind it, which Pel could not hear through the rain.

The door unlatched and opened, revealing an attractive vedzryyf'len in maid's attire.

"Can I help you?" she asked.

"I'm Father Pel," the paladin replied. "I'd like to speak with Sir Dumentyn."

The vedzryyf'len's eyes widened, and she swung the door wider.

"Oh, Father! I'm terribly sorry. Please, come in. I'll inform the master."

Pel stepped inside, half-expecting something shideic to lash out at him, but it never came. The maid closed the door behind him and walked away.

He took off his hat and placed it on a nearby bench. As he began to quietly unbutton his coat, he examined the opulence of the home. Expensive wood with intricate carvings adorned the trims of the rooms and railings of the stairs.

After he had taken off his coat, another maid came to take it and his hat. He thanked her and gave them to her. She bowed and walked out of the hallway.

Pel agonizingly waited before the vedzryyf'len came back. She bowed.

"Follow me, Father," she said, and turned.

He noticed she was a nynbyrle'len. Her hair was tied into a working bun, revealing a copper disk in each of her ears.

He followed her through a room and down a hall to a door. The woman stopped at it.

"He's waiting for you inside," she said, motioning to the door.

Pel's brow furrowed in concern. She did not open the door for him; she just stood there. He looked at the doorknob hesitantly. Then, he grasped it and opened the door.

It swung open without a sound as he stepped into the room. Looking beyond the door's border, Pel found the room to be a massive study. A large space occupied the middle of the room where a star pattern was made from the floorboards. Bookcases lined the walls, and Sir Dumentyn sat at a desk at the far end of the room.

"Father!" the man said, standing up. "To what do I owe this visitation?"

Pel quickly looked around for anything that seemed out of the ordinary. He found something.

"I've some questions to ask of you," Pel replied.

"Well, come! Come sit down," Sir Dumentyn said, gesturing to a pair of chairs on the side of the room.

Pel acquiesced. As he walked gingerly toward the seats, he noticed the star in the middle of the room was unfinished, but would have eleven points when done. A stack of pre-cut floorboards sat near it.

"Having the floor put in?" asked the paladin.

"One of the azurns damaged it," the other said, sitting down in a comfortable chair. "Dropped a glass of brandy."

Pel sat down in the opposite chair, the bright gas lamp drowning out the light in his eyes.

"Must've been a tough glass to damage wood," he said.

"Only the finest." Sir Dumentyn paused. "Going to battle?"

"Excuse me?"

"The sword."

"Oh! I've heard there's been a rash of attacks lately."

"I have heard that as well. Dreadful." He paused. "Care for a drink?"

"No, thank you."

The man poured a drink from a decanter and took it in his hand.

"Now, Father, you had some questions for me," he asked, taking a sip of the amber liquid.

"I do," Pel replied.

"What about?"

"Dzokaya."

———◆———

Dzokaya sat silently on the bed in her small-clothes. She had been there since Pel locked her in the room, some time ago.

"I hope he is alright," she said to herself.

The girl eyed the Uch Rynahl next to her. She had never read it as she thought it never pertained to her. She was half vedzryyf'len; her Mother was Ar'ka Mohn, not Qia Mora. But the girl remembered what Pel had told her when they met, that *his* Mother did not practice nor preach the enslavement of vedzryyf'len.

She grabbed the book and opened it to the first page. There, a dedication was written in a feminine script: "For my love. May you find peace in the Order."

"Alteya," the half-breed read.

She closed the book and her eyes.

"Mother...guide me."

Her horns buzzed.

She opened the book to a random page and read: "And Qia Mora said to Ar'ka Mohn, Go and craft Your Daughters and I My Sons, and they will each other love so to raise an army against Yych Rehe[1] should he again rise."

Dzokaya's horns buzzed fervently, as if Ar'ka Mohn Herself was telling her she read the truth. She lay the book on her lap and thought.

Her life had been filled with ridicule and disgust. She had never been treated as an equal, though her mother had taught her how to level their enemies. But Dzokaya had never once done it; she thought it unlady-like. As well, her father reminded her of their status and its fragile standing. Her father had never put much stock into it, but his occupation was worth something to people whose heads he could hold it over. Dzokaya was always hamstrung by her need to be a lady; in fact, it was her mother who taught her how to control her temper, and her father taught her how to be a diplomat between men.

And in her time in Corlia — a haven of the vedzryyf'len slave trade — she came to see how those of her kind less

---

1. (EEX REH-huh) A corrupted entity that is seen as being Qia Mora and Ar'ka Mohn's mortal enemy. He is responsible for the creation of the shiden, whom he commands as his armies.

fortunate than she were treated and behaved. She wanted to do something to help them, but, being a highborn, it would destroy her father's reputation; if she had done anything, he would be known as a prominent banker whose half-breed daughter led the hornless in a revolt — he would be exiled.

Would that have been better? she thought.

Then, a notion struck her like lightning. How did her *mother* feel? Dzokaya was only half vedzryyf'len, but her mother *came* from Mohnaht — she was full-blooded. How much did *she* have to restrain herself? Dzokaya recalled her mother telling her to behave for the love of her father, so she behaved. *Mother must have loved him so much if she did not do anything before.* In fact, before her untimely death, her mother seemed the *least* offensive of the three; the woman never seemed to draw the ire of anyone. She was always courteous, and bowed and curtsied when she was supposed to. She had assimilated into society — at least outwardly. At home, her mother had kept some Mohnahti traditions alive, and her father seemed not to care. Indeed, Dzokaya failed to remember a moment when her mother carried her sword in public, or anything that would peg her for holding onto her home country; she must have done it on purpose.

To save Father's image?

No, it was not just that; she must have loved Dzokaya's father so much that she would do anything to make him look better among his peers. Searching her memories, Dzokaya knew she did. When her father appeared forgetful, her mother took the blame. When her father seemed to be undisciplined, her mother came up with an excuse as to why — usually to her detriment. When her father came home drunk, it was her mother who cleaned up the mess. *For love?* she thought.

Yes, it was for love. But she thought about what *she* would do for love. Immediately, her parents stepped into her mind's eye. She would avenge them, even if it took her life.

My life.

Pel's sacrifice came to mind. Not only did he die for her — albeit risen by Qia Mora — but he locked her in the room to protect her. He did not do it for the same love she had for her parents; rather, it was the love a Son of Qia Mora had for a Daughter of Ar'ka Mohn. Dzokaya came to realize that that love should drive her to protect *him*.

Her eyes open, Dzokaya stood up, the holy book dropping off her legs to the floor. She rushed to the door and grabbed the knob, pulling it. It did not budge. She looked around the small room for anything that could help her with the door. Then, she eyed the pile of her wet clothes on the desk, with something poking out from underneath. With a confused brow, she stepped forward and pulled off the clothes. Lying on the desk sat her unsheathed sword. A smile sprung upon her face as she gazed upon its blackness.

Thinking quickly, she rushed to the armoire and searched for clothes.

After a short time, Dzokaya was dressed in girl's clothing. She grabbed the blade and dragged her fingers across its flat. Then, she faced her palm toward the door, projecting a dark shockwave from her hand and blowing the door open. She rushed out of the room and down the stairs to the den. The girl grabbed a woman's coat off a hanger and threw it around herself. She unlatched the door and, taking a deep breath, went out into the rain with her sword strapped to her waist.

———◆———

Pel and Sir Dumentyn sat in the study, the latter with a drink in his hand.

"Dzokaya is quite the girl," Sir Dumentyn said, swirling his drink.

"She is," replied Pel. "How do you know her?"

"Her father and I work — *worked* — together."

"What's your line?"

"Banking," the man said, swallowing a sip. "Quite prolific, actually."

"I'm told you're from Corlia."

"The *business* is there, yes. *I* am Riahlish."

"Really?" asked Pel, leaning back. "Where do you hail from, exactly?"

"I was born in Orentor[2]. But my family moved here — to this very house — after Cesren[3] Koliad was elected."

"So, why not pursue banking here? Why Corlia?"

"Well, the slave trade," the banker said, leaning back and crossing his legs. "Cannot invest in it *here*, as you know."

"Of course. But what's the bank got to do with it?"

"It's a front."

"I see."

"It's quite lucrative, really," Dumentyn said, taking another sip. "Believe it or not, Riahls will pay a hefty price for Corlian slaves."

"So I've heard," Pel said with a stern countenance, as if expecting the man to take the conversation into an inappropriate direction.

"But Dzokaya's mother — and Dzokaya by circumstance — hindered that a bit."

"I can imagine, being vedzryyf'len."

"It's a shame, to be honest, that they had to die."

"What do you mean 'had to die?'" Pel said with a raised eyebrow.

Sir Dumentyn stared at his drink as he swirled it slowly in his hand.

---

2. (OR-ehn-tor) The central state of Riahla, home of the nation's capitol, Methryget.

3. (SEHSS-rehn) Title of the leader of Riahla. Equal in role to a nation's president.

"Father," he paused. "May I...confess my sins?"

"Of course."

———◆———

Dzokaya ran through the streets as the rain assaulted her face, and the wind tossed her hair. She had to fly if she were to face her parents' killer with Pel — to get revenge. The girl held her sword's hilt tightly in her grasp as she ran.

She knew she had to go south to the Beach District to get to Sir Dumentyn's home; she knew that area well. Each flash of lightning illuminated the street signs, giving her a sense of direction.

A flash illuminated a sign: West Sereth Street.

"Almost there," Dzokaya said to herself as she rounded a corner, heading west.

———◆———

Pel sat quietly, waiting for Sir Dumentyn's confession. The man seemed nervous, if only slightly, and he rubbed his hands on the drinking glass.

"I had Dzokaya's parents—" he paused. "The Erenleths were...murdered." He said the last word slowly, as if struggling to get it out.

"*You* killed them?" a surprised Pel asked.

"*I* didn't. No."

"But you made the decision."

"I...hired someone, so to speak."

"Sir Dumentyn, speak plain," Pel said cautiously.

Suddenly, there was a rumbling coming from under the floorboards.

"The slave trade was so profitable. I couldn't have them stop me."

"Speak plain, Sir."

The rumbling intensified, as if growing closer.

"Had they turned me into the Riahlish authorities, I would be arrested," said the banker nervously. "I had no other choice."

"Speak...plain," Pel said firmly.

The floor shook more.

"I *had* to do it."

The rumbling was violent, now. Pel stood up swiftly.

"Damn it, man! Speak plain!"

Suddenly, from the center star on the floor, erupted a cloud of black and white smoke. A growling steam engine emanated from it.

———◄O►———

As Dzokaya came to her destination, she breathed heavily from her exertion. She walked up the stoop as the torrential rain fell upon her. When she grasped the knocker, she knew: the shid was on the other side. The girl was suddenly nervous. This was it.

She knocked several times and waited.

After a few moments — though for the drenched Dzokaya, it felt like hours — the door opened.

"Dzokaya!" said the maid before she ushered in the half-breed. "What are you doing here?"

"Where's Sir Dumentyn?" the girl asked hurriedly.

"Let's get you out of these—"

"Where is he?!"

"He's in his study."

Dzokaya suddenly bolted for the backroom. The maid tried to stop her, but was too slow. The girl would not faint this time.

◈

Pel stood stunned as he gazed into the gaping, drooling maw of the shid. A steady, low growl came from its invisible throat. Then it spoke in a language Pel now recognized, but though he did not know the words, he understood their meaning.

"Priest!" the shid said in a deep, sinister tone. "You live." It snarled as it sniffed the air. "You stink of Qia Mora."

Pel unsheathed his sword, which unleashed a blade of glittering gold and silver flames. He looked at it in surprise, then stood steadfast, grasping it in both hands.

"She has blessed you," the shid said.

"And you have been *damned*," Pel replied.

"Once. Not again."

The shid projected a tendril at Pel to impale him again. The paladin stepped aside and slashed it, cutting it off in a sizzling burn. The evil creature recoiled in pain, screaming. The cut end of the tendril smoked and smoldered.

The monster sent out another tendril, and Pel cut it down, eliciting another pain-filled roar from the beast.

Suddenly, the door to the study flew open, with Dzokaya on the other side. The shid threw out a tendril and slammed the door on her.

"No!" Pel exclaimed.

Dzokaya grabbed the doorknob and tried to open the door, but it would not budge. She unsheathed her sword and dragged her fingers across its flat, then unleashed a dark pulse from her palm. The door blew open, surprising all within.

Sir Dumentyn — who was cowering until now — stood up and pointed at the girl.

"Kill her!" he commanded.

The shid turned its attention to Dzokaya and threw several tendrils at her. She pushed the sword in front of her, creating a dark barrier that blocked them.

Pel rushed the shid, which tried to push him away; he cut away the arms and slashed at the shid's mouth. The fiery edge split open its chin, the gash glowing hot and spurting out black sludge. The beast recoiled again and pushed Pel away with an aethereal shockwave; he flew back, breaking the table that he was sitting at before.

Touching her sword, Dzokaya slung forth several dark bolts at the maw, chunking away its disgusting flesh. The shid tried to shake off the pain, but the girl continued the onslaught.

Sir Dumentyn stood near Pel as the paladin got to his feet.

"You can't defeat it," the banker said with a quivering voice. "Submit to it."

"I submit *only* to Qia Mora," the paladin replied before he ran at the monster with his sword raised high.

The banker watched as Dzokaya and Pel fought the shid. As they slowly cornered the evil fiend, Sir Dumentyn saw a glimpse of his salvation. If they could destroy it, he would be free of its aethereal hunger and repent.

The three remained still, as if waiting for the other to make a fatal move. The shid emitted a low growl as it contemplated its next action, but it would not have to wait long.

Pel rushed it, and as it centered its attention on the paladin, Dzokaya leaned back and slid the palm of her hand across the flat of her sword. Then, in a swift motion, she projected the sword out of her hands toward the shid. The creature saw the weapon flying at it, but at the same time, Pel moved to attack. The shid attempted to block both, but failed, its power no longer a suitable replacement for its skill. Dzokaya's blade embedded itself into the upper jaw of the fiend, and Pel's flaming sword was thrust into its lower jaw, the tip sticking out of its flailing tongue.

The shid lit up in gold and purple flames, thrashing its many tendrils and reeling in cacophonous pain. Pel dislodged his sword from the creature and stepped back. The shid cursed in its language as it slowly sank into the floor as a ship would in an ocean.

"I will not go alone!" it exclaimed.

In near lightning speed, it threw a ghostly tendril at Sir Dumentyn, which impaled itself into the banker with no real effect. Then, like something out of a horrific nightmare, the shid retracted its transparent arm, with a ghostly version of Sir Dumentyn attached to it. The apparition was gone as quickly as it had appeared. The body of the banker collapsed.

As the last of the creature submerged into the floorboards, it released a grotesque cry.

"Yych Rehe will get his revenge!"

Then, in a blast of black and white smoke, the shid disappeared. The half-breed's blade lay where the creature had been, glittering dark blue and violet. Dzokaya and Pel stood still, breathing heavily.

The girl shook, but she stood fast. After a moment, she walked over to her blade and picked it up. She examined it, then pressed the point into the wood where the beast had descended; it was solid.

"It's gone?" Pel said through heavy breaths.

"It is," Dzokaya said, pausing. "But not dead."

Pel sheathed his weapon, extinguishing the flaming blade, and walked over to the girl. He put a hand on her shoulder.

"Did you get what you came for?" he asked.

Dzokaya looked at the corpse of Sir Dumentyn. It was shriveled and dry, like her parents were that day. She knew.

"Almost," she said, sheathing her sword. "I wish *I'd* been the one to kill him," referencing the banker.

Pel sighed.

"Perhaps another day," he said, referring to the shid.

She understood his meaning.

"No," Dzokaya replied solemnly. "I don't think that day will come."

Pel's brow furrowed.

Dzokaya sounded different. Her accent had softened somewhat.

The two turned around to see a handful of house staff standing in the doorway, eyes wide. They knew the house workers had seen what happened.

"Tell no one," Pel said.

The staff just nodded.

Pel and Dzokaya walked out of the room without another word.

As the two walked out of the house, they looked up to see the dark clouds that had hung over the city slowly dispersing, allowing the sun to spear through them. Pel smiled.

"It seems we've done it," the paladin said to the girl.

Dzokaya looked at him with stern eyes.

"So it seems," she said before she started down the stoop. Pel slowly followed.

"What will you do now, Fath— *Lord* Pel?"

He continued to smile at her and rested his hands on the pommel of his sword.

"First thing is I go back to that tavern and clear out my things."

"I mean after that," Dzokaya asked innocently. "Once you've left and all?"

He looked down at his sword, then chuckled.

"Would seem Qia Mora has a mission for me yet," he said.

"So, you *are* a paladin?" she asked, sounding almost disappointed.

"I am."

"Then I suppose I'll never see you again."

"Perhaps only in dreams," said Pel. He put his arm around Dzokaya's shoulders and led her down the road. "What about you? *Your* mission's done."

"Perhaps from the outside," she replied. "That shid isn't dead."

"Not sure you really *can* kill a shid."

"The point is," she paused, "I did not avenge my parents. I didn't take what was mine." Dzokaya sulked.

"But you sent it back from whence it came. And it took its slave with it."

She pulled away from him.

"But that was *my* task to do," the girl shouted with tears in her eyes. "That was *my* responsibility!"

"*Your* responsibility is to live," Pel shouted back, like a father scolding his child.

The girl was quiet.

"I don't know *your* parents, but I know *parents*," Pel started. "And the ones I've met would *never* approve of what you tried today." Dzokaya stood silently, expecting him to say something wise or prophetic. "They *always* wish for happiness. I can't imagine *yours* would be happy."

Dzokaya dropped her head and started to cry. Pel took her in his arms, their dampness mingling into something that made her sorrow even worse.

"I tried," she said through tears. "I tried."

"And you succeeded, as far as *I'm* concerned," replied Pel, his chin resting on her head. "Listen. This wasn't my first fight."

"You've fought shiden before?" Dzokaya sniffled.

"Well, no. This was my first fight with a shid. *But*, I've been in battles. Sometimes, when your enemy retreats, it's to avoid absolute failure and become stronger. And sometimes they *are* stronger the next time." Pel pulled them apart and looked into Dzokaya's sad eyes. "But *you* will be stronger, too." Dzokaya sniffled and wiped her eyes. "I saw you fighting. You're not magister level, but it's a start."

"I don't know *how* to get stronger," Dzokaya sobbed.

"Clearly...you have to learn from a vedzryyf'len. Where are vedzryyf'len?"

"Corlia?"

"Not slaves. *Free* vedzryyf'len. Ones with horns, like yourself."

"Riahla?"

"No, there's not enough of them here. You need to go where there's *a lot* of them."

"Mohnaht?"

Pel smiled.

"Mohnaht. Go to Mohnaht."

The two continued to walk down the road: his arm around her shoulder, and her arm around his waist.

9

HIS NEW CALLING

AS THE STORM CLOUDS dispersed and sunlight began to warm the city streets, Geth Rell started to come alive. People walked the cobblestones and cabbies rode to their usual pick-up spots. Indeed, within hours, the city was replete with activity.

After their battle, neither Dzokaya nor Pel had an appetite — except to be rid of the place. As they said their goodbyes to Kyf and Toya, an old man with an equally-old staff walked up to them. His spacious robes hid a lean body, his face and knobby hands being the only indications a human was under them. His face was wrinkled, with a large raptor beak-of-a-nose and thin lips. His eyebrows were long and fluffy, and matched his beard and long hair in their hoary color.

The four stood confused by him as he greeted them.

"Pel," he said in a gently croaking voice. "Dzokaya."

"How do you know us?" Pel asked .

The old man smiled.

"I have been watching you," he replied with a strange accent. "Seeing what you've done." He paused. "You, and the events of today, have gotten the attention of my lady."

"And who might *that* be?"Kyf asked.

"I cannot tell *you*, Kyffryn Rettyk. But these two," the old man said, gesturing to the two meigys users, "are the only ones to know."

Pel gestured for the couple to leave. They stood off to the side, just out of earshot.

"If I may ask," Pel said, "who *are* you?"

"Ar'l Kah[1]," said the robed man. "I am an advisor of Cesren Kyrdeleth."

"Your lady, though. The Cesren's no woman."

"His *wife* bids you join her."

"His wife?"

Ar'l Kah nodded. There was a moment of silence.

It was unusual for the wife of a Cesren to take on any official political duties. But if Cesren Kyrdeleth's wife asked for them specifically, she must have need of a paladin and vedzryyf'len, Pel reasoned. The paladin turned to the girl.

"Are you willing to go?" he asked her.

---

1. (ahr-uhl KAH) Advisor to past and present Riahlish governments. Those in his inner circle know him as the Myyren'geth (Literally "Agents' Brother," but more accurately "Agents' Ally"); the relevance of this term is unknown by mortals.

Dzokaya looked at Ar'l Kah with a skeptical squint.

The man was tall, and he exuded a powerful aura the girl could hardly ignore. It was a swirling of ancient meigys, the likes of which she had never seen. But she was sure as ever that while the figure who stood before her was human, his aura was certainly not.

"I suppose," Dzokaya replied stiff-lipped, still maintaining a skeptic's gaze.

"Very good, then," said the old man.

"Do you have a coach?" asked Pel. "I don't see one anywhere."

"Those are too slow," replied Ar'l Kah. "I prefer...meigys."

"I'm not sure I understand."

"Teleportation does not work that way," Dzokaya said.

The man looked down at Dzokaya, whose comparative size was that of a toddler.

"For you," he said.

Suddenly, a shining blue-purple light emitted from the top of Ar'l Kah's staff. Then, it flashed brightly, blinding the four before him. When the light dissipated, Kyf and Toya opened their eyes, and the other three were gone. The couple stood wide-eyed.

"Who was *that*?"Kyf said.

The sun shone brightly on the field of the Cesren's Mansion. It was an old building, dating to before Riahlish Unification, but it had been updated to keep up with current fashions — at least internally. It was large, but not large enough to have one think some wealthy businessman spent his absurd earnings on a lavish living space. Instead, it looked very much like an old magistry school, which it was.

Centuries before the founding of Riahla — before the Shiden War — the magisters who were far more powerful then had set up an exclusive academy to train future magisters. After the decimation of the magisterian elite, the school no longer had the prestige to continue, and the newly-united Riahlish government required a residence for its leader; thus, the Cesren's Mansion was established.

There was a short stoop that led to the double-doored entrance, and two magisters stood at attention there on either side, armed with their rapiers. Suddenly, a cloud of crackling blue-purple energy appeared before them, and the trio appeared. The magisters seemed unaffected by the unusual occurrence.

"What happened?" Dzokaya exclaimed.

Pel looked about himself, then at the building before him.

"We're in Methryget!" he said, astonished.

"Where?"

"The capitol."

"How did you get us here?" asked the confused girl.

Ar'l Kah turned to her.

"Like I said," he replied, "teleportation does not work like that...for *you*." He looked at the two near him. "Are you ready?"

The two collected themselves, then both agreed that they were.

"Follow me," the sage said.

The man stepped up the stoop, and the doors swung open unaided ahead of him. The paladin and the half-breed followed closely behind him; how they followed him, however, could not be more different.

Dzokaya followed Ar'l Kah closely and sternly, her mind like an adding machine trying to make sense of her observations. Pel, on the other hand, did not know where to look first. He had never thought he would ever get to see the inside of the Cesren's Mansion; such a feat was only for politicians and war heroes, however few there were left of the latter.

After a while, a staircase, and another while, the group arrived at a set of ornate doors. Pel recognized they depicted the destruction of the eight nations with the first Cesren and Riahla rising out of the ashes relief-carved out of solid hardwood. As they approached, the doors opened.

Inside, Cesren Kyrdeleth sat at his desk, three men standing before him. He eyed the new guests between the arms of the men who were pestering him, and stood.

"Master Kah," said the Cesren in an energetic tone.

The three men separated to give the man a view.

"Cesren," replied the sage.

"Ulja is looking for you," the man said. "Please. Use my office." He started to round the desk. "Gentlemen, let us continue this in the cabinet room."

The four men exited, closing the doors and leaving the three meigys users alone in the office.

"The Commanding Office," Pel said in amazement. "I never," he said, setting himself down on a couch.

Dzokaya sat beside him.

"I didn't expect you to be so awe-struck," she said, smirking.

"I wouldn't expect you to understand."

"Indeed. I've held no allegiance to a country."

"Not even your own?"

"I never felt it was mine to begin with. Being such an outsider—" she paused.

"Though you were inside," Pel finished. He exhaled. "I can't say I know the feeling. But I understand it."

Suddenly, the doors opened and in came a woman — older than Toya, but hardly by much. She stood in a typical feminine dress, with an open-buttoned women's jacket. The long, poofy skirt hid a pair of formal women's heels. She was attractive in a mature fashion, and had Pel not seen a photograph of her, he would have thought of her as a high-end madame. Her dark hair cascaded over her shoulders and down her back, locks of white hair framing her face.

The doors closed as Pel and Dzokaya stood.

"Master Kah!" said the woman, taking his huge hands into her own. She looked at Pel and Dzokaya, then back at the sage. "These are them?" she asked gaily.

"Yes, Milady," Ar'l Kah replied.

The woman smiled and moved to Pel and Dzokaya as they stood up.

"I am Ulja Kyrdeleth, High Lady of Riahla," she said. "And you are?"

Pel hesitated.

"Dzokaya, Madam."

They shook hands.

"Just call me Pel, M'lady," the paladin said, putting out a hand. They shook hands.

The High Lady sat across from the pair on an opposite couch, a coffee table sitting between them.

"Would you like me to leave you alone, Milady?" Ar'l Kah asked.

"No, no," Ulja replied, still looking at the shid slayers. "You should stay."

"I have to ask—" started the paladin.

"No," the High Lady interrupted, "it is *I* who must ask." She paused. "Was it truly a shid you fought?"

Pel and Dzokaya looked at each other in hesitation.

"I assure you, no one will hear of this aside from us four," Ulja said.

After a moment of silence, Pel spoke up.

"It was," he replied.

"Then it is worse than we thought," said the High Lady to the sage.

"M'lady," said Pel, "why have we been called here?"

Ulja sat straight and placed her palms on her lap.

"Pel. Dzokaya," the woman started, "I would like to recruit you to be Riahla's personal shiden vanquishers."

The pair sat stunned. Pel's brow raised, while Dzokaya's fell.

"I know it is unexpected," Ulja said.

"Indeed," Pel replied. "What's led to this...decision?"

"Ar'l Kah and I have been collecting...occurrences throughout Riahla where shideic influence is suspected. I am not happy to say that the collection is vast and varied."

"Why not enlist the help of Her Chosen? Veteran paladins?" Pel asked.

"We have," replied the High Lady. "They have no reason to suspect shiden are here due to the power of the Barrier. They attribute such occurrences to insanity and hysteria."

Pel sighed, and Dzokaya remained silent.

"As a new paladin, I'd have to go to them anyway. I could request their aid when I do."

"I hope they *would* aid you," Ulja said.

"Or they may not," said Ar'l Kah.

"What do you mean?" Pel asked.

"Yes, friend. Explain."

"Before the Cormorian Formation, a paladin appeared in what is now Yrczreth[2]. After he sent the shid back to Yych Rehe, he sought training at the Academy of Her Chosen[3]. They turned him away, citing the Barrier."

"Did he have the Gaze?" Pel asked.

"Yes. He even displayed his power. But they thought it was a demonstration of some advanced magistry, again citing the existence of the Barrier."

"What happened to him?"

"He disappeared," Ar'l Kah replied simply.

"Could you find him?" the High Lady asked.

The sage stood quietly.

"I...know where he is," he said after a few moments.

"You do?" said Ulja. "Why did you not tell me? I could have requested *his* help."

"Because *I* asked for his strength," said Ar'l Kah. "He declined."

"Declined? Why?"

---

2. (ER-chrehth) The northeastern state of Riahla that butts up against the Northern Barrier Mountains.

3. The institution that governs paladins explicitly, and the only human power they are required to follow; rogue paladins have been known to be executed by the Academy.

"He was told to cease activity some time ago by the Paladins' Council." The old man paused. "Or he would be labeled a heretic."

"Something tells me he was anyway," Pel said.

"Dzokaya, my dear," said Ulja, "you have been awfully quiet. What have you to say?"

Dzokaya looked at each face that awaited her response.

"I find...this doesn't concern me," the girl said.

"I do not understand," said the older woman.

"Riahla is not my country. I'm a foreigner, an outsider. This matter of shiden in your nation is not mine to deal with." She stood up and bowed. "High Lady Ulja, it was an honor to meet you. But I must be on my way."

Dzokaya walked out of the room, leaving everyone surprised. Pel stood and rushed to the door.

"Excuse me," he said.

He went out of the room and hurried to follow the girl.

Pel called out to her in the halls as he followed far behind her, but she did not answer. He followed her outside, where he found her standing at the bottom of the stoop.

"Dzokaya!" Pel called, walking down the steps. "Dzokaya."

"Don't try to convince me, Pel," she said, turning to face him.

"I see there's no use in trying," he said. "You've made up your mind, then?"

She nodded.

"I have."

"Then I'll have what's-his-face come out here to get you back home."

"Very well," Dzokaya replied, standing straight, her hand on the hilt of her sword.

Pel walked over to her and put out his hand.

"Good luck in Mohnaht," he said.

Pel was surprised to be suddenly embraced by the half-breed girl, her face buried in his chest. He closed his arms around her.

"Thank you," she said, pulling her face away from his now-wet shirt. "For everything."

Pel smiled at her and wiped the tears from her cheeks.

"I'd do it again if it came to it," he replied.

She smiled and released him, wiping her eyes.

"I hope we meet in more than just dreams," she paused, "and on a happier occasion."

The paladin turned and walked back into the building.

When the door opened to the Commanding Office, Pel met the High Lady and Ar'l Kah with a forlorn smirk.

"Sir," he said to the sage, "she'd like you to take her home," he finished, pointing his thumb behind him.

"Of course," the old man said. "If I may, My Lady?"

She nodded.

Ar'l Kah left the room, closing the door behind him.

"Is she alright?" the High Lady asked.

"She is," the paladin said as he sat down. "She has her own journey to go on that doesn't involve us *or* Riahla."

"I see." High Lady Ulja paused. "What about you, Pel? Will *you* aid us?"

Pel leaned forward, placing his arms on his knees and clasping his hands loosely.

"I will...on one condition."

"What is it?"

"I was a soldier present at Gendytha Point. I saw men — good men — commit a heinous act because they were told to do it." Pel paused, his eyes fixated on his interlocutor in a steely gaze. "I will do no such thing under your command." His voice was serious, a hint of past anger vaguely apparent. It did not get past her.

"I understand," replied the High Lady, returning a resolute countenance. "Although I...command you, as you say, I will leave solutions to these incidents for you to determine at *your* discretion."

"Thank you, M'lady."

"Once Ar'l Kah returns, I will instruct him to take you to the proper authorities. I hope they can help you."

"Tell me, M'lady, who *is* Ar'l Kah? He has meigys that doesn't exist — or *shouldn't* — exist."

High Lady Ulja briefly looked down at the table before her in thought. She returned her eyes to Pel's inquisitive face.

"He is at least as old as the the Great Mother and Ar'ka Mohn, and probably just as powerful."

"Then why doesn't *he* take care of the shiden?"

"He is instructed not to lend mortals his power."

"*Instructed?* By whom?"

Ulja shrugged.

"He has not told me, but already we know too much. He has been an advisor for Riahla since before Unification[4]. His counsel has been invaluable to our people."

Pel sat back and put a fist to his chin in thought.

"Please, Pel. Stay focused *only* on the shiden you must exorcise from our nation. Yych Rehe seeks to uproot our world. He seeks vengeance on Our Lady and Her sister. You *must* stop him."

---

4. High Lady Ulja is referencing the Riahlish Unification, which took place shortly after the Shiden War but before the Cormorian Formation.

DEAR READER

Thank you for joining Pel and Dzokaya on the first leg of their journey!

What happens next:

Pel has accepted his calling as the Sovereign Guardian, but divine power means nothing without training. As instructed by High Lady Ulja, he seeks out the first paladin of Riahla to learn what it truly means to be Her champion. But the shid he and Dzokaya faced is far from dead; it's plotting in the darkness, and time is running out.

Dzokaya, meanwhile, has chosen her own path to power. In Mohnaht, her training will take her to hidden tribes who knew her mother, and who harbor secrets about her bloodline that could change everything.

Their paths have diverged. But the darkness gathering will force them both to become something greater than they ever imagined.

Book 2, *Fall of the First Champion*, arrives Q1/2 2026.

Want early access? Join my Substack at https://jordanekristofer.substack.com for exclusive updates, character insights, and a sneak peek at the opening chapter.

Loved the story? Reviews help other readers discover Pel and Dzokaya's journey. Every rating matters, especially for independent authors.

Follow the journey: Instagram @ymran218 for writing updates, fantasy art, and behind-the-scenes looks at Cormoria.

The story continues. I hope you'll be there when it does.

~Jordan